Guy Fraser was born in Scotland and has an MA in Ancient History and Classical Archaeology from Edinburgh University.

A PLAGUE OF LIONS

1863. Superintendent Henry Jarrett, formerly of the Hong Kong police and now Chief of the Detective Department at Glasgow Central, is comfortably ensconced in Elsie Maitland's superior guest house for single gentlemen. However, the tranquillity is short-lived when a major bank robbery calls for the attention of Jarrett, Inspector Charlie Grant and Sergeant Tommy Quinn. Then, the undermanned department has a series of gory murders, an attacker who lies in wait for maids on their night off, and a cold-blooded poisoner. Stretched to breaking point, they can well do without the activities of a confidence trickster and his loyal assistant . . .

Books by Guy Fraser
Published by The House of Ulverscroft:

BLADE OF THE ASSASSIN
JUPITER'S GOLD

GUY FRASER

A PLAGUE
OF LIONS

Complete and Unabridged

ULVERSCROFT
Leicester

First published in Great Britain in 2009 by
Robert Hale Limited
London

First Large Print Edition
published 2010
by arrangement with
Robert Hale Limited
London

British Library CIP Data

Fraser, Guy.
  A plague of lions.
  1. Police- -Scotland- -Glasgow- -Fiction.
  2. Murder- -Investigation- -Scotland- -Glasgow- -
  Fiction. 3. Glasgow (Scotland)- -Social conditions- -
  19th century- -Fiction. 4. Detective and mystery
  stories. 5. Large type books.
  I. Title II. Series
  823.9′2–dc22

  ISBN 978–1–44480–328–0

Published by
F. A. Thorpe (Publishing)
Anstey, Leicestershire

Set by Words & Graphics Ltd.
Anstey, Leicestershire
Printed and bound in Great Britain by
T. J. International Ltd., Padstow, Cornwall

This book is printed on acid-free paper

1

The first indication that something was wrong came as Superintendent Henry Jarrett was about to start breakfast. Normally the dining room at Mrs Maitland's superior guest house for respectable single gentlemen could boast of being sedate, even funereal, except when the overweight Albert Sweetman took it upon himself to comment on the state of the world. But at least on this particular Monday morning it would be blessedly brief, since the travelling partner in Hall and Sweetman, Wholesale Ironmongers, had already announced that he was about to set off on a tour of the Borders. There, he let it be known, he would undoubtedly pick up some excellent orders and not a few outstanding accounts.

'We have acquired a new agency,' Sweetman told chemist Wilbur McConnell, when it was clear that Jarrett, as always, was paying him no mind, preferring instead to direct his attention to Mrs Maitland's excellent kedgeree, which would be followed by thickly cut toast, uniformly tanned and evenly buttered, and a pot of Keiller's marmalade. This, and his favourite Ti Kuan Yin Black Dragon tea, a taste for which he had acquired during his years in the Hong Kong police force, made for him the perfect breakfast. Undeterred by Jarrett's complete lack of interest, Sweetman continued, 'Etna Foundry's products. We are particularly hopeful for their cast-iron grave markers.'

Wilbur McConnell smiled weakly.

'Is that to keep the body snatchers out or the deceased in?' he asked.

If there was one thing Sweetman hated it was someone else being funny. So he ignored the chemist's attempt at humour and instead jerked his head in the direction of the empty table by the window.

'The Croall fellow still absent, I see.'

Henry Jarrett sat back in his chair, produced his silver hunter and flicked the case open. It was a gesture he had often performed when he thought matters were getting out of hand. The implication being, of course, that time ruled all things and there was no need for idle chatter. He was just as curious as the others as to why assistant bank manager Croall had been hurriedly called away without so much as a bite to eat or a mouthful of tea, but he had no intention of indulging in pointless speculation.

'He left the house quite urgently, I believe,' McConnell offered. 'A Hansom arrived for him about seven-thirty, but I'm afraid the maids are being less than forthcoming about the whole thing. It's all very mysterious.'

After Sweetman had departed to prepare for his trip to the Borders, Henry Jarrett had the distinct feeling that the reticent chemist was trying to summon up the courage to speak to him. But at length the man also took his leave, nodding to Jarrett as he went, and clearly having decided that whatever it was he was desirous of saying could wait. For his part, the superintendent was only just keeping to time as he finished his kedgeree and started on the toast. The Ti Kuan Yin, as always, was exactly right, having been made with water that had come off the boil for a full minute.

Elsie Maitland, as expected, appeared in the doorway of the large dining room, having first made sure that both Sweetman and McConnell were well out of earshot over the crest of the steep stairs, then came quickly across the cherry-red expanse and placed a hand on Jarrett's shoulder.

'I am not supposed to know this,' she whispered, 'but there has been a major incident at the Western Bank. Mr Croall is in a terrible state.'

The superintendent nodded and inclined his head slightly to catch the first distant

3

sound of hooves and iron-rimmed wheels on cobbles. As they became louder he rose from his seat and patted Elsie Maitland's hand before it dropped from his shoulder. Never a demonstrative man, that was as far as it went without the key being turned in the lock.

'Jamieson, unless I miss my guess,' he said. 'Probably late tonight.'

'The girls and I will still be up,' Mrs Maitland said softly, 'whenever you arrive.'

PC Jamieson tipped his driver's cap as Jarrett climbed on board the wagonette, then wheeled Domino around and set off down Delmont Avenue to its junction with Highfield Road.

'Western Bank, Byres Road, sir,' Jamieson offered, but that much Jarrett had already guessed.

'What's it all about, Jamieson?' the superintendent asked after a few moments.

Usually, such prompting would have been quite unnecessary, but the police driver was somewhat reticent on this occasion and not in his natural forthcoming state.

'Called me a dolt, sir,' he said huffily. 'Said he might as well talk to Domino.'

'This will be Chief Constable Rattray, I suppose?'

'I'm afraid so, Superintendent. I know I

am not permitted to criticize a superior officer —'

'Then don't do it, Jamieson. You have my sympathy, but standards have to be maintained. That can mean swallowing humble pie and being respectful, even when the other side is not.'

Jamieson smiled happily and was immediately his old self again. He could never imagine Henry Jarrett speaking to subordinates the way Rattray had spoken to him, not to mention his treatment of Inspector Grant and Sergeant Quinn.

'Thank you very much, sir,' he said and meant it.

'Well now,' Jarrett said, as he watched the great plane trees in Kelvingrove Park skimming past and wished he could devote himself to nothing more complicated and demanding than strolling happily with the one lady in his life. But until he retired problems would arise on a daily basis and moments of relaxation would have to be snatched as and when it was possible, 'how bad is it?'

'They tunnelled in, sir. If you'll excuse my French, it's a hell of a mess.'

'The safe?'

'No, sir, the private boxes. It's the big ones who have been hit this time, superintendent.

5

The ones who have something to lose and don't like it.'

'God almighty.' Jarrett shook his head grimly. This was not going to be his best day. Which meant that he was not in the mood for one of Jamieson's nuggets of edification.

'This used to be a village when my grandfather was a wee boy,' the police driver announced, obviously back to his old self. 'Byres of Partick, they called it.'

'To the best of my knowledge,' Jarrett replied, 'everywhere used to be a village.'

Inspector Charlie Grant was waiting on the pavement in front of the large double doors of the Byres Road branch of the Western Bank. Like Jamieson, he had been taking a great deal of verbal abuse and was only just managing to keep himself under control. Rattray's recent return from a slaughtering holiday, during which he murdered everything that swims, runs or flies, did not seem to have improved his general demeanour. Charlie Grant, for his part, was obliged to accept the fact that God did not endorse prayers about hunting accidents.

'I think you should brace yourself, sir,' Grant said, but somehow managed a faint smile through it all. 'They've struck at the very vitals of the city.'

'I gather it is the safe deposit boxes.'

'Absolutely. Pays to have bugger all sometimes, doesn't it, Superintendent?'

Jarrett gave him a dirty look, partly because of the highlander's impudent comment, but mainly because the CC's private carriage was still sitting there. He had dared to hope it might be gone.

Rattray, his silver-topped cane stabbing in the air as he barked orders to all and sundry, and generally added to the confusion, turned on Henry Jarrett as soon as he entered the foyer.

'So there you are!' he yelled, but thought twice about actually prodding the superintendent with the cane. That had been tried in the past and had not been well received. 'How in God's name could such a thing happen?'

'I really couldn't say, sir,' Jarrett said. 'I was asleep at the time.'

Rattray's face darkened as he closed in on Jarrett.

'I will not be spoken to in that manner,' he growled. 'You forget yourself, Superintendent.'

'My apologies, sir, but the sooner we get started the sooner we can get on the trail of those responsible.'

'Are you accusing me of being in the way?'

'Are you, sir?'

The CC was shaking now, and both

Inspector Grant and Sergeant Quinn, to Jarrett's right and left, were briefly concerned that their chief had gone too far this time. Then Rattray pushed his way through and past them, pausing only when an attendant opened the door for him.

'I need to be kept informed, Jarrett,' he shouted. 'A lot of important people are going to be pressuring me non-stop, so don't for a moment think I won't pass it on. I want results and I want them soon.'

Once the CC had gone and the large doors were again closed to keep out the curious, most of whom had little personal interest in the bank or its problems, Henry Jarrett said, 'Lead on, gentlemen. I must be the only one around here who hasn't seen the work of art for himself.'

The secure room lay at the end of a long corridor and was entirely hidden from the eyes of the day-to-day customer. Access to it was by means of a heavily barred door which was now wide open to permit the comings and goings of the staff and investigating officers. Even before he reached the ragged hole in the terrazzo floor, Jarrett could see the extent of the physical damage. Each of the eighty brass-hinged mahogany boxes had been burst open and cast against the end wall. Adding to this jumble were the

8

numerous documents, some crumpled, some torn, which the thieves obviously had no need for.

'Deliberate chaos,' Jarrett said flatly. 'This was done to slow down our enquiries. To state the obvious, until the bank finds out what is missing we don't know what to look for.'

'Perhaps Mr MacPherson can give us some idea about that,' Inspector Grant said, indicating a small, bewhiskered gentleman with enormous sideburns and a bald pate, who was at that moment advancing on them with the familiar James Croall in tow.

'Lawrence MacPherson, branch manager,' he stated in a way that suggested a long history of speaking down to people while looking up at them. 'Mr Croall tells me that you are Superintendent Jarrett, the senior officer. I really must insist on there being some progress before the day is done.'

'Why today in particular?' Jarrett asked coldly. He had to accept it from the CC, but not from this one. 'Do you have any idea of what exactly we have to do?'

'I know what is expected of you, just as I know what is expected of me. For your information, Superintendent, as soon as we arrived to discover this calamity I tried to contact the box holders through a front page advertisement in the *Advertiser*, but I was too

9

late. Printing was under way. I therefore had no alternative but to send an urgent telegram to the affected parties. This at my own expense, you understand, although I am not a wealthy man.'

'My commiserations, Mr MacPherson.'

'I don't want your commiserations.' The little man waved in the general direction of the team of clerks as they scurried back and forth with trestle tables, which others then assembled in two long rows. 'Apart from a small number of box holders who are currently abroad, I am anticipating a deluge of irate customers very soon. They are for the most part members of the carriage trade, sir, and accustomed to the highest quality service. I am now going to have to assemble whatever pitiful items were left behind in the hope that we can find out what is missing. In the process, of course, I will have to take endless abuse.'

Jarrett had been quietly nodding at all the appropriate places. Then he asked, 'What sort of things are likely to be missing?'

'Anything of value that is not immediately required by the box holder. A wide variety of documents, bonds, jewellery, rare coins and so forth.'

'Cash?'

'No.'

Jarrett gave this a few moments' thought.

'I believe that some banks keep ledgers for those clients who wish to declare the contents of their boxes.'

'Correct, but we do not.'

'In that case they will lie to you. You know that, don't you?'

MacPherson stared at him in horror.

'I object to that remark,' he blurted.

'Then you are a bigger fool than you look, Mr MacPherson. I am not a betting man, sir, but I'll wager half of them will have lost granny's jewels.'

'That's a preposterous allegation.'

'Mr MacPherson, my only interest is in ensuring that my men do not waste their time searching the jewellery shops and pawnbrokers for non-existent valuables. So what I suggest is that a couple of detectives join your staff at the tables. That should tone the proceedings down a little and it might even result in an outbreak of honesty.'

Mr MacPherson's lips moved but nothing came. Suddenly, he turned on his assistant and snapped, 'Croall, recover those documents and try to make them as presentable as you can. Hurry up, now.'

But by then Jarrett was no longer interested in what he had to say. Instead, he was kneeling by the edge of the hole and admiring

11

the villains' handiwork.

'It isn't high enough to pass through easily, sir,' Sergeant Quinn offered. 'You can see it better from the shop.'

Two doors to the north on Byres Road, and separated from the Western Bank by a pastry shop, the property with a blank sign space had, according to the various beat policemen on this stretch, lain empty for about three months. Just under a fortnight ago the window and door glass had been painted black behind wooden shutters, making it impossible to see inside from any vantage point. But since this was hardly illegal, and indeed was not an uncommon practice with undertakers, it was merely assumed that this was to be the latest attempt at making this particular site pay.

As soon as it was established that this was the source of the tunnel, uniformed officers acting on Charlie Grant's orders had broken open the heavy padlock and gained entry to the darkened interior. Grant and Quinn had already given the place a cursory examination, partly to meet any questions Jarrett might throw at them, but mainly to get away from the Chief Constable. They had also lit two oil lamps found in situ, and placed one of them where the shop would best be illuminated and the other in the tunnel.

The first thing that was apparent was the level of neatness and order compared to the chaos of the bank's inner vault. The clay and boulders that had been removed while tunnelling had been piled up against the rear wall of the shop, and the tunnel itself, although only some three feet or so in height, was regularly and evenly shored up. Resting on the wall facing the tunnel mouth were two short-hafted pickaxes and two equally dumpy shovels. Other items used in the work included a large wooden bucket, a hammer and a large cold steel chisel. All of these objects, being no longer required, had been grouped neatly together in a corner as though to taunt the investigating officers.

'A professional job,' the superintendent said. 'The complete blackout would have prevented even the slightest glimmer of light from the tunnel being seen by the officer on the beat.'

'Miners?' Charlie Grant offered.

'It would look that way.' Jarrett paused briefly, then said, 'Suggestions, gentlemen. Your thoughts on the subject would be most helpful.'

'I think we can safely say the digging was carried out by night,' Tommy Quinn advanced. 'I have no idea how long it would take to excavate a tunnel forty or so feet long and just over a yard in height and width, but it had to pass under the pastry shop to reach the bank and I would guess that they would have been heard if they tried it by day.'

'Good point. I would put their number at around three, perhaps four. There isn't room for two at the face, so I would reckon on a digger, a labourer removing the spoil from the work and another squirreling it out of the tunnel and piling it up. There might have been someone supervising the activities and listening for the night beat's tackety boots, but that would be all. Any more than that and they would be falling over each other.'

'I can't argue with any of that, sir,' Inspector Grant admitted. 'I would go for a non-participating intelligence behind this operation, either your fourth man overseeing everything or someone safely elsewhere and waiting for results.'

'I would say he was here,' Sergeant Quinn said. 'Two reasons, Superintendent. The tunnel was very carefully measured so that they would come up exactly in the middle of the inner vault passageway. That required a considerable degree of accuracy. Also, who-ever rifled the safe deposit boxes knew exactly what he was looking for.'

'Just as the bank manager said — precious items, artefacts, coins and so forth.'

'Precisely. As you observed, sir, the mess they made of the documents was intended to slow us down. Contrast that with the orderly way they worked this place.'

'True, but it doesn't help us a great deal to know we judged them accurately. Without knowing what we are looking for we stand little chance of catching these men.'

'I don't think that's what the Chief Constable is waiting to hear,' Grant said. 'We're going to have to be seen to be doing something, Superintendent, even if it's just playing at silly buggers.'

'Until we can find one pointer, one single clue, however tiny it may be, that is precisely what we are going to be doing. The trick is not to make it look like that, so you can start by finding out as much as you can about every branch employee, from the doorman to MacPherson.'

'You think they had inside information, Superintendent?'

'Right now, Inspector Grant, I'm not really thinking anything.' Jarrett turned then to the young Irishman. 'Sergeant Quinn, I want you to find out who shared the night beat here and tell them to report to me immediately. Also, check the files, solved and unsolved, for some reference to tunnelling or a related occupation.'

15

'What could possibly be related to tunnelling, sir, other than tunnelling itself?'

'I'm damned if I know, but we have to start somewhere. And if Rattray corners you tell him we are following up a positive lead.'

'If that isn't good enough, should I say we expect to make an arrest in the near future?'

'Do that, Sergeant, and you'll be on the first boat back to Dublin,' Jarrett said, frowning, 'and so will we.'

At that moment Charlie Grant jerked a thumb in the direction of the greater world.

'That sounds like the first of the carriage trade arriving,' he said. 'Looks like MacPherson's nightmare is under way.'

'Then I had better go and join him,' Jarrett said. 'You can't begin your investigation into the bank's employees while this fiasco is in progress, Inspector, so in the meantime I would be obliged if you could find the owner of this shop and who, if anyone, rented or leased it in the recent past. And while you're at it, you might like to enquire as to why the people in the house upstairs didn't report anything.'

2

In the mind of Elsie Maitland, it seemed almost as though some form of largely unspoken understanding had existed between her and Henry Jarrett, and that it had begun on the very day and hour he arrived at 76 Delmont Avenue. It concerned their united future and guaranteed special treatment for the head of the Department of Detectives, which he gracefully accepted and unashamedly exploited. But that was the level of attention expected by the former chief of the Hong Kong police. So without its actually being put into so many words, it was accepted by both parties that in the perhaps foreseeable future Superintendent Jarrett's not inconsiderable savings and considerable pension would combine with the realized value of 76 Delmont Avenue and the as yet undisclosed sum Ernest Maitland left behind when he dropped dead in the street. Indeed, just about the only thing Jarrett did tell Mrs Maitland was about his inclination for a largish property somewhere on the coast, and that he had a particular fondness for Largs. In saying this, of course, he assumed that she would wholeheartedly agree.

One positive indicator of her acquiescence was a growing tendency to consult him on matters that, strictly speaking, were her domain. She had done so on the question of hiring a second girl for kitchen duties, and now had sought his opinion on the matter of heating the bath water. She had already converted what was once a ladies' changing room into a bathroom for her paying guests, but Lizzie and Jeannie still faced the onerous task of heaving numerous buckets of scalding water upstairs every time one of the gentlemen was in need of a dip. A gas geyser would, Jarrett pointed out, be the logical solution. A new-fangled gadget, perhaps, but he had heard nothing but good of them as far as their operation was concerned. And it would be much cheaper to install than running hot water pipes up from the boiler to the second floor. The only possible area of contention would be the actual cost of heating the water, and that invariably fell upon the guests. But although landladies had experienced a certain amount of grumbling, that was generally short-lived and everyone soon came to appreciate the benefits of progress.

And that was why Benjamin Carney, Plumber and Gasfitter, drew his cart to a halt outside the front gate and proceeded to lower the rear flap of the vehicle, while his apprentice, Kenny Noone, dumped a ringed iron weight on the pavement and tethered the horse's reins to it.

'Shift it, laddie,' Carney called. He had drawn the hefty Etna copper and iron geyser as far towards himself as he dared without risking it landing on his toes. 'Give a hand here.'

Elsie Maitland sent Jeannie to open the garden gate for them and now waited expectantly by the front door while the workmen staggered up the sea-washed pebble path with their black-japanned contraption.

'Where would you like it, missus?' Carney asked and young Kenny giggled. It was his regular try-on, which almost always passed harmlessly by, but on very rare occasions produced the response he wanted to hear. This was not one of those times.

'Top of the stairs and to the left,' Mrs Maitland said, her eyes following closely the progress of the heavy metal contraption as it passed between the door jambs. All exterior woodwork had been recently copal-varnished and she was not about to brook the slightest dent or scuff. 'Watch how you go, now.'

With Kenny leading backwards and Carney having to brace himself to compensate for

Kenny's left-handedness, they got the Etna geyser as far as the half-landing before pausing for a breather. In Elsie Maitland's opinion this was quite unnecessary, and if they had not come on recommendation she might have seriously doubted their worth. But they were soon on their way again and in due time reached the door to the bathroom, where they were instructed to wait until she joined them and supervised the final stretch. Here the woodwork was primarily white with the beading picked out in black. Once again, no dent or scratch would be tolerated.

Nor would having this heavy object sitting on her upstairs hall carpet. They had to hold it up until their arms ached and their legs began to buckle, while Lizzie and Jeannie folded a heavy cotton sheet four times to make a suitable mat for it to rest on.

'Well, now,' Mrs Maitland stated. She wanted the improvement, but not the fuss. And certainly not the mess. 'Exactly how long will it take you? I would like you out by midday.'

'So would I, missus,' Carney said.

★ ★ ★

Henry Jarrett left Detective Constables Williamson and Russell in attendance at the trestle tables and was back in his office at Central by noon. Tommy Quinn's search of the files for some crime-related mining enterprise had produced absolutely nothing, despite the fact that it seemed like a logical way to gain access to a bank. There were four instances of robbers breaking through a common wall and one of access being obtained through the ceiling, but this was the first real mole job in this city at least. Other police forces might have had different experiences, particularly London, but that remained to be seen.

But at least Quinn had fetched PC Corrigan and PC Kane, both of whom were waiting outside in the oak-panelled hallway, their eyes on the wall opposite and their hair neatly moistened with soapy water and brushed into a crisp parting. Considering they had both been asleep when the call came, and had only a matter of minutes to get up and get out, they were neatly turned out in the chequered Sundays and glossy boots. Despite the fact that both had excellent records, always met up with the sergeant on time and had never been warned about imbibing on duty, they were fearful of the sack.

Since Corrigan had been on the five till midnight shift he was called first and was surprised to be offered a seat.

'You know about the robbery at the Byres Road branch of the Western Bank?' Jarrett asked.

'Only that there was a break-in, sir.'

'More accurately, the thieves entered the premises through a tunnel that started two shops to the north. What I want to know, Constable, is whether you saw anyone enter or leave that particular property.'

Corrigan's response was immediate.

'Early Thursday evening, Superintendent,' he said confidently. 'A gent alighted from a Hansom and was unlocking the shop door just as I passed.'

'Did you speak to him?'

'In a friendly sort of way, sir. Since his future business was going to be one of my charges I was naturally interested to know what it was.'

'What did he say?'

'It was to be a flower shop, I understand. He has a nursery on the South Side.'

'Almost certainly a lie from start to finish. Constable,' Jarrett observed, but noted it anyway. 'I can't imagine this lot of criminals being foolish enough to give anything away.'

'My apologies, Superintendent. Perhaps I should have reported it to the sergeant.'

'You had no reason to do so.' Jarrett gave

this some thought. 'Was that your only contact with the perpetrators.'

'No, sir. I saw the same man again on Saturday evening, but although I acknowledged his presence I didn't actually speak to him on that occasion.'

'But you are sure it was the same man?'

'Absolutely, sir.' Corrigan's controlled expression remained in place. 'It was him all right.'

'Can you describe him?'

'Nothing outstanding, Superintendent. Gent, but otherwise average in every way.'

'By gent, you mean not dressed like a labourer?'

'And the way he spoke, sir. I wouldn't exactly call him cultured, sir, not like a toff, but certainly educated and accustomed to talking.'

'Age?'

'Late thirties or thereabouts, sir.'

'Clean shaven or moustachioed?'

'Clean shaven apart from sideburns.' Corrigan paused, then added, 'There was a faint scar above his left eye, sir.'

'Well observed, Corrigan. That could prove valuable.' Jarrett added this detail to his so far unconnected list of facts. 'Now, are you familiar with the staff of the Western Bank?'

'Not really, sir, no. To be honest, I've rarely

had any cause to enter the building. There was a slight disagreement a few months ago when I was doing days, but it was only a minor misunderstanding and easily settled. I got the impression that the last thing the management wanted was a policeman on the premises. Bad for business, I suppose.'

Henry Jarrett smiled.

'The only other thing I would like you to do, Constable, is accompany Detective Sergeant Quinn to the Western Bank and take a look at the staff. It isn't likely that the man you spoke to in the doorway is a bank employee, but we have to be sure.'

Constable Kane, on the midnight till seven shift, would not have been expected to encounter anyone entering or leaving the shop. Rather, Jarrett's questions concerned unusual sounds in the vicinity of the bank or shops. Twice, according to Kane, he thought he heard a sharp sound which might have been nocturnal activity in the tenement houses above the commercial row. Someone moving a brass bed around, perhaps. Since he could not imagine anything else it might have been, he put it down to a domestic situation of sorts and did not report it to the sergeant. An unfortunate decision, perhaps, but only with the benefit of hindsight and as such not a disciplinary matter.

The man was tall, gaunt and utterly humourless. He hovered over the trestle table like a vulture waiting to pounce, and even Detective Constable Russell was slightly unnerved by his threatening presence.

'Did you touch these?' The voice was soft and rasping. 'Did you handle them?'

Russell looked down at the four wooden squares and the ancient calfskin wallet that had once contained them. Each tile, if that was what they were, measured about six inches square and was deeply carved with a religious scene of sorts.

'No, sir,' Russell said honestly. 'Would it matter?'

'It would matter very much.' The man fixed him with a cold stare. 'Do you know who placed them here?'

'Absolutely no idea, sir. Perhaps Mr MacPherson might be able — '

'Don't bother. It was with the best of intentions I'm sure.'

Russell glanced at Williamson, but there was no help to be had from that quarter.

'Presumably these belong to you, Mr — '

'Brand. Cyrus Brand, Parkfield House.' The gaunt man indicated a tied sheaf of yellowing papers. 'And those too. Thank God the vandals didn't destroy them.'

'What about valuables?' Russell asked. 'Can you tell me what you may have lost?'

'A few items of sentimental value. Heirlooms of no great worth.'

'Nevertheless, it might help us catch the villains, Mr Brand, and that is what we all want to do.'

'Yes, of course.' Brand gave the matter some thought. 'There is a gold lion brooch that is quite distinctive. Plated, I believe, but if you see that for sale you'll be left in no doubt as to what it is and where it came from.'

At that moment Mr MacPherson put in an appearance and greeted Brand in a manner that confirmed the thin man's position as an honoured client.

'What can I say, Mr Brand?' he said in his best funereal tone. 'It is nothing short of a catastrophe. How could we possibly have anticipated such an act?'

'Well, no doubt you will in future, Mr MacPherson. Meanwhile, I have no doubt that the good Lord will deliver the culprits into the hands of the law.'

★ ★ ★

They assembled in Superintendent Jarrett's office to pool their information and try to think of something that might appease Chief Constable Rattray, or at least hold him off for a little while longer. Trouble was, he had nothing to do up there but traverse between his oversized desk and his equally oversized window, and on every round trip his patience, never good at the best of time, grew steadily thinner.

'First,' Sergeant Quinn said apologetically, 'PC Corrigan did not recognise any member of the bank staff. The man in the shop doorway certainly wasn't one of MacPherson's clerks.'

'I didn't really hold out much hope in that department,' Jarrett admitted. 'What about the property above the shop, Inspector Grant?'

'Well, one house spans both the empty property and the pastry shop next door. It is one of several houses owned by a Mrs Charlotte Stuart of Langfield Mansion in West Regent Street and administered by Hillyard and Palmer, property agents and house factors. It was occupied by James Frowley until a month ago, then lay empty for only a week or so before Benjamin Laird rented it from the factors.'

'Have you spoken to this Mr Laird?'

'That's the point, sir. When I couldn't find anyone who knew Laird and couldn't gain access to the house, I had one of the uniformed men put his shoulder to the door. The place was absolutely empty. No sign of habitation at all and scarcely a stick of furniture.'

'So Laird is almost certainly one of the gang.'

'Unless I miss my guess, Superintendent, he is the one Corrigan spoke to and is either the brains behind the whole thing, or at least in charge of the operation and answerable to a higher power.'

'At least we have his description, so that's something. Have you found out who the gang rented the shop from, because it must have been done through proper channels.'

'I sent Detective Constable Bryce to make enquiries. The woman in the pastry shop confirmed that she pays rent to Hillyard and Palmer, the house agents who represent Mrs Stuart. Unfortunately, she doesn't know if this woman also owns the empty shop.'

'Good. In the meantime, there are four possible areas of investigation open to us. I want someone to talk to the Hansom drivers, on the off-chance that one of them can remember taking the man who calls himself Laird to the empty shop. If we can find out where he was picked up that would be better than nothing.

'Next, assign two or three men to covering pawnbrokers, salerooms and jeweller shops, particularly those known to have handled stolen goods in the past. I know it's a bit early, but there is just the possibility that the criminals tried to off-load their ill-gotten gains immediately. We have an artist's sketch of the gold brooch reported to Detective Constable Russell, so get that photographed and printed off a couple of dozen or so times. If dealers know we are looking for this piece in particular they won't touch it, but they might just notify us if and when it is offered to them.

'Now this option is probably pointless, but I would like your views on it. Since we agree that this is almost certainly the work of experienced miners, is there anything to be gained from visiting all of the pits in the area to see if anyone can offer useful information.'

Charlie Grant shook his head.

'Too many pits, Superintendent,' he said. 'Lanarkshire is full of them. The closest would be Strathbungo, where there are hundreds of men to be considered.'

'All right, we can get Corrigan to describe the dubious Mr Laird to the artist and circulate the picture, with the scar emphasised, to every pit manager in the district. And while you are at it, it occurs to me that you might try to find out how long it would take to excavate a tunnel such as the one used by the robbers. Also, are we correct in our estimate of the men who may have been involved? What do you think of that?'

'Much better, Superintendent, and it would please His Nibs to know that we are on a positive trail.'

'Agreed.' Jarrett directed his attention to Tommy Quinn. 'Sergeant, you assign men to the cabbies and arrange for an artist's likeness of Laird.'

'I know it is extremely unlikely, sir,' Inspector Grant offered, 'but it might be worthwhile to talk to the factors, Hillyard and Palmer, and perhaps also the owner, Mrs Stuart. I don't think there's one chance in a thousand that our fictitious Mr Laird gave a genuine former address when he took on the rental of the house and shop, and even less of a chance that Mrs Stuart is behind the crime, but it is worth a try.'

★   ★   ★

Langfield Mansion turned out to be an elegant three-storey mid-terrace house in West Regent Street, between Douglas and Pitt Streets. Henry Jarrett was admitted by a small, wizened sort, who appeared to have

30

outlived his butling days and would almost certainly now be described as a retainer. This, however, spoke well of Mrs Stuart, since there were many who would have dumped the old boy on the human midden when he could no longer be trusted with valuable breakables.

'We have always had a rather peculiar attitude to property,' Charlotte Stuart said, gesturing to a large chair she wished Jarrett to occupy. He had declined her offer of tea on the grounds that the visit would be a short one and there was much to attend to. 'For all their great wealth, many of the early tobacco barons like my great-grandfather still lived in gloomy tenements like everyone else. It was only later that the craze for building mansions and villas began.'

'It is actually property that I specifically want to talk to you about,' the superintendent stated. 'I understand you own a house in Byres Road.'

'No, I own several houses in that district. Which one are you interested in?'

'It is a three-roomed apartment above a pastry shop and another retail establishment that is currently empty.'

'The shops are also mine, but there shouldn't be an empty one. My factor, Mr Hillyard, let me know a few days ago that the former plumber's store had been taken for a flower shop.'

'We believe that to be a ruse, Mrs Stuart. Advance rent was paid, but the person concerned had no intention of opening a flower shop or anything else. He and his cohorts merely wanted a secure site from which to tunnel into the Western Bank two doors away.'

Mrs Stuart sat forward abruptly, clearly shocked by this revelation.

'Good Heavens,' she gasped. 'Who — '

'At this precise moment I'm afraid I cannot divulge any further information.' Jarrett did not, of course, admit that he didn't have any, but it was often useful to suggest otherwise. 'Do you have any information you feel might be of interest?'

'No.' She shook her head and seemed briefly bewildered, but soon rallied. 'Except — '

'Mrs Stuart?'

'It's my brother, Christopher Hadden. He hasn't been home for two days and I am more than a little concerned.'

'Presumably your brother stays here with you?'

'Yes, he moved in after my husband died. That was just over two years ago. We were always close. Orphaned in India, you see. Fever.'

'Is he in the habit of going missing?'

'No, this is the first time. He isn't what you might call a gregarious man. He is a member of the Steamboaters' Club, but apart from that I wouldn't say he had many friends.'

'And that is?'

'A group of like-minded individuals who spend their weekends sailing up and down the Clyde, although God alone knows why. I was on one of those things once and that will do me.'

'Some of them are really quite plush.'

'And some are floating deathtraps under the command of crazed captains who try to break records, regardless of their passengers' welfare.'

Jarrett could scarcely argue with this.

'Perhaps Mr Hadden is on a trip to . . . wherever.'

'He would have told me first. And anyway, he doesn't sail during the week.'

'Perhaps his employer could enlighten us. What does Mr Hadden do for a living?'

Mrs Stuart shrugged lightly.

'He doesn't work,' she said. 'He is a retired army officer, which makes it all the more surprising that he should be more interested in steamboats than military matters. Most men in his position are members of the Greys or the like.'

'Business interests?'

'He has two directorships. The Woodside Coal and Shale Company, and MacQuaid's Shipping Company.'

The absence from home of Christopher Hadden, coinciding as it did with the bank robbery, was probably the first real lead Jarrett had, but before he could pursue it he required one vital piece of information.

'Does your brother have a scar above his left eye?' he asked.

She looked quizzically at him, but answered nevertheless.

'Why, yes,' she said, 'and another on his left shoulder. They were caused by a kukri.'

Although Jarrett found the lady quite pleasant and would normally have wished her no ill, it was cheering to know that he at least had a name to give to the Chief Constable at their next meeting. It was better than shuffling on the spot.

'Tell me Mrs Stuart,' he said, 'did Mr Hadden ever have any dealings with your agent, Hillyard and Palmer?'

'I don't believe he did. Christopher doesn't take much to do with day-to-day matters.'

'So Mr Hillyard wouldn't recognize him?'

Mrs Stuart frowned.

'What are you suggesting, Superintendent?' she asked.

'I am not suggesting anything, merely exploring every and any possibility.'

'In that case the answer is no, he probably wouldn't know Christopher. My brother never visited the factors' office and Mr Hillyard does not come here. If we need to communicate with each other, a letter sent in the morning will reach its destination by noon, which is as quick as anyone requires.'

To Superintendent Henry Jarrett, who had eagerly embraced the electric telegraph and looked forward immensely to the day when it would be installed in every home, Mrs Stuart's old-fashioned attitude was quaint and charming.

★ ★ ★

'Christopher Jordan Hadden,' Jarrett told Inspector Grant and Sergeant Quinn later. 'Forty-three years of age, five feet ten inches in height and of slim build. He has a small scar over his left eye and another on his left shoulder as a result of a disagreement with a kukri. It goes without saying that he is almost certainly the Mr Laird who rented the house and shop, and the man PC Corrigan spoke to in the doorway. There can be no doubt that he is the leader of the group.

'Also, he holds two directorships. The

Woodside Coal and Shale Company, and MacQuaid's Shipping Company. The former points to where he obtained the diggers, and the latter suggests that he may at this moment be leaving the Clyde Estuary for the high seas.'

'Would you like me to check MacQuaid's ports of call, Superintendent?' Tommy Quinn asked.

'No need. They are transatlantic. I doubt if he would be making for America, at least until the War Between the States has been concluded, so I think Canada is the most likely destination. It goes without saying that our chances of locating him if he moves west are not good.

'However, first things first. Inspector Grant, you take the MacQuaid's Shipping Company. Find out all you can about Hadden. And while you are at it, check the passenger lists of any sailings within the last few hours as well as those about to depart. It would be nice to think that he was still here and that we could get this whole thing wrapped up very quickly.

'Sergeant Quinn, take Williamson and Russell with you and call on the Woodside Coal and Shale Company. I am not sure how you are going to approach this, but the aim is to identify the men who constructed the tunnel. Of course, it is perfectly feasible that none of the Woodside miners had anything to do with it, but if they had not this is one coincidence too many.'

By now, it was late afternoon and Henry Jarrett found himself thinking about dinner as he always did around that time of the day. Mrs Maitland, God bless her, had whispered that it would be chopped lobster patties with roast potatoes and apple fritters. That was very much to his liking and he could only hope that her plumbing improvements went according to plan, or it might turn out to be cold collation instead.

For the time being, however, all thoughts of dinner and relaxation would have to be pushed to the back of the mind, because Chief Constable Rattray was waiting for his report. At least now there were two definite leads and the prospect of a satisfactory conclusion, which was more than Jarrett had to offer the last time he climbed the stairs to the eyrie.

★　★　★

The girl strode purposefully along a path that was becoming dimmer by the minute. Although the sun was still a good distance from the horizon, down here at the foot of the gentle slope the trees grew thickest because they were closer to the gently winding stream. Once or twice she stopped and looked behind her, thinking she had heard a sound. It was possible, of course, that it could be an animal of sorts, and she was thankful that there were no dangerous creatures, such as wildcats and the like, in these parts. She had been told that a badger will deliver a nasty bite if anyone or anything is blocking its run and preventing it from reaching its sett, but then that could be said of just about anything, humans included.

Then it struck.

One hand clamped her mouth; the other gripped the handle of a short knife, the point of which bit into her throat. The voice, indistinct and ageless, was muffled by a thick scarf wrapped around the attacker's face. It warned her against the stupidity of resistance. In her blind panic clear thought was impossible, and only the most basic desire to survive remained.

3

Breakfast. A time for garnering the thoughts and planning the day. During his sojourn in Hong Kong, this was Henry Jarrett's favourite meal, but then he didn't have to share his space with other diners. However, for once it came close to the tranquillity of his bungalow in the Fragrant Bay, because Albert Sweetman was somewhere in the Borders, selling his ironmongery and collecting out-standing monies. Apart from making a pest of himself with the maids, that was Sweetman's primary purpose in life.

And there was another notable absentee. James Croall, assistant manager of the Byres Road branch of the Western Bank, had been called away yet again, this time not long after sunrise. It would seem that several of the box holders had not yet provided adequate proof of their ownership of various discarded documents and other miscellanea from the smashed safe deposit boxes. Mr MacPherson, now all the more anxious for his own future with the institution, was demanding that all of his staff be in attendance along with him. He was the captain, and as such morally obliged to go down with the ship, but apparently he was damned if he would go down alone.

Anticipating this, Mrs Maitland and the girls had risen early, provided Mr Croall with a decent morning repast and made up a lunch box in case he couldn't get out of the building. The superintendent could only hope that the colourless little man appreciated the trouble the good lady had gone to on his behalf. Many a landlady would have let him go without if he couldn't meet her timetable.

That left only Wilbur McConnell between Jarrett and blessed isolation. Like Croall and unlike the gregarious and rather crude Albert Sweetman, the chemist was a quiet, unassuming individual, who rarely spoke and tended to keep himself largely to himself. But at that moment Superintendent Henry Jarrett just knew that Mr McConnell was going to break with tradition and cross the large cherry-red carpet to broach whatever matter was troubling him. He had come close to doing so the previous morning, but his nerve had failed him at the last moment. Jarrett didn't necessarily consider himself to be so unapproachable, but it often looked as though others did.

As was his wont when the last piece of toast

had been consumed, the superintendent fished out his silver hunter and consulted it. Just ten minutes until the Menzies tartan bus was due to leave for town, so if McConnell had anything to say now was the time to say it.

The chemist rose from his chair, headed for the doorway to the hall, then turned on his heels and made a beeline for Jarrett.

'Superintendent,' he said cautiously, 'I wonder if I might have a word with you.'

'Yes, of course.' Jarrett bade him be seated on the other side of the small table. 'What is troubling you, Mr McConnell?'

'I fear I may have unwittingly been a party to a crime.'

'Really? And what sort of crime might that be?'

'Murder.'

The superintendent folded his napkin and laid it aside.

'Perhaps you should start at the beginning,' he said.

'Yes, perhaps I should.' McConnell chose his words carefully. 'Perhaps I exaggerated when I suggested that I was an actual party to murder. I should have said that I was injudicious.'

'In what way?'

'Well, several weeks ago a gentleman came

into my shop and purchased three shillings' worth of arsenic. He explained that it was to kill rats in the cellars of his city hotel and accordingly signed the poisons book.'

'He must have a serious rat problem,' Jarrett observed, 'but it is still perfectly in order.'

McConnell smiled thinly and reached into his waistcoat pocket, from which he produced a newspaper cutting. This he laid before Jarrett, then sat back and waited until the superintendent had read it.

'As you can see, Superintendent,' he said, 'it is the funeral notice of Jacob French, who died last Wednesday at the age of seventy-three.'

'A not unreasonable age,' Jarrett observed. 'Are you suggesting he was unlawfully killed?'

'If you look at the list of mourners you will see the name of Alexander Bisley second from the top. That was the name in the poisons book, Superintendent Jarrett. The first mourner is Jacob French's sister, Seraphina Bisley. She is the mother of Alexander and the rightful inheritrix of the French estate.'

'Which is presumably considerable?'

'Very considerable.'

Jarrett folded the cutting and, having indicated by holding it up that he would like to keep it, put it carefully away in his fob pocket.

'Unless I miss my guess, Mr McConnell,' he said, 'you believe that Jacob French was hurried out of these mortal coils by his nephew, Alexander Bisley, so that Mrs Bisley could collect the estate. The next logical step in this chain of events is that Mrs Bisley herself will contract some serious complaint and likewise be taken out feet first.'

'I can see why you are the chief of detectives,' McConnell observed. 'But yes, that is exactly what I fear. The similarity in the names is too great and the timing too close for the arsenic to have really been bought for the purpose Bisley claimed it was.'

'It is an interesting notion, Mr McConnell,' Jarrett said, 'especially as there wouldn't be a post-mortem on a man of that age.'

'Not only that, but Jacob French was suffering from heart disease and was expected to die sooner or later. It is my guess that Alexander Bisley, for whatever reason, merely brought forward the final date.'

'With no great risk to himself.'

'Exactly.'

'Tell me, Mr McConnell, how do you know about Mr French's condition?'

'When I became suspicious of Bisley, I made it my task to find out all I could through enquiries in the trade. Things get about, you know, especially from travellers who move from one shop to another all day long. I only had to ask four or five salesmen if they had ever heard of Alexander Bisley before one of them told me he was Jacob French's nephew and that he worked for his uncle in the Commodore Hotel in Gordon Street.'

'That is good work, Mr McConnell,' Henry Jarrett said, briefly consulting his watch once more and discovering that he had a mere five minutes to reach the horse-bus terminus. 'I will make enquiries, of course, but it may turn out to be a completely innocent set of circumstances. At least I hope it does.'

'As do I.' Wilbur McConnell rose when it became apparent that Jarrett was about to depart. 'I hope you don't think I go around poking my nose into other people's affairs, Superintendent.'

'Anything but. You did exactly the right thing, Mr McConnell, but I would now ask you to keep your suspicions to yourself and leave further enquiries to us.'

★　★　★

It was the very last thing Tommy Quinn expected when he arrived at Central Police

44

Headquarters. He glanced briefly at the stern-looking woman and the girl who were sitting on the public bench directly across from Sergeant Black's desk, but forgot them almost as soon as he passed by. Until Davie Black waved him across, that is.

'Just the very man, Sergeant Quinn,' Black said, beckoning him closer in confidence. 'It's a ravishing.'

Quinn glanced over his shoulder.

'The girl?'

'Megan Speirs, maid, fifteen years of age.'

'Is that the mother?'

'Employer. Miss Emily Monk. Needless to say, the girl would have run a million miles rather than be here, but Miss Monk knows better, so here they are.'

'And here I am,' Tommy Quinn said softly. 'I don't suppose — '

'All too busy, I'm afraid.'

'Inspector Grant?'

'Oh, far too busy.' Davie Black gave him a knowing wink. 'Keep this to yourself, Sergeant, but they think this is one area of operations you need some experience of.'

'Did they say that?'

'Not in as many words, but you can tell. They reckon you need a baptism of fire, and as far as I'm concerned, rather you than me.'

Tommy Quinn had almost reached them

before they looked up at him.

'I'm Detective Sergeant Quinn,' he said, hoping it sounded sympathetic.

'You're Irish,' Miss Monk pointed out needlessly.

'Yes.'

'And Romish.'

'Yes.'

'Better than nothing, I suppose. I am Miss Monk and this is my maid, Megan Speirs.' She indicated the pasty-faced girl with a careless flick of a gloved hand. 'She won't say much, so you may address your questions to me, but I would be grateful if you could keep them brief and tasteful.'

'It is scarcely a tasteful subject, Miss Monk,' Tommy said, trying to hide his growing irritation. 'Now, if you would like to come with me at least we can conduct the interview in private.'

★ ★ ★

Henry Jarrett and Charlie Grant paused in their discussion and acknowledged Tommy Quinn's arrival at the superintendent's office.

'How is she?' the superintendent asked.

'Shocked. I couldn't get much out of her. Not that I stood much of a chance with Miss Monk there.'

46

'What did you find out?'

'The girl joined Miss Monk at the age of twelve, straight from Dame School. There are no other servants, and I got the impression that it isn't the usual sort of relationship.'

'Meaning?'

'They share a room.'

Jarrett nodded. 'Not illegal,' he said. 'Restrictions about that sort of thing apply only to the male of the species.'

'Quite so, sir, but what exactly — '

'Don't even ask, Sergeant. Between us, Inspector Grant and I have stumbled through half a century of police work without a clear understanding of certain matters. What I do know is that this animal has to be run to ground. Question is, where do you start, bearing in mind that you are still involved in the Western Bank robbery.'

'Yes, I know, Superintendent. To be perfectly honest, it is hard to know what to do. I gave Miss Monk an assurance that we would do everything in our power to catch the character, while at the same time knowing that there was just nowhere to start.'

'Not exactly nowhere, Sergeant,' Charlie Grant put in. 'Look at Grace Martin's file. It was about three weeks ago. There may be a pattern, and if so you have something at least to go on.'

When Tommy Quinn had gone off to compare the details of Megan Speirs's assault with those of Grace Martin, Inspector Grant picked up the thread of the earlier conversation.

'I sent Detective Constable Drummond round to Hillyard and Palmer, Superintendent, and the front office clerk gave him a description of Benjamin Laird that was as close to the man PC Corrigan spoke to in the shop doorway as makes no difference. It was his likeness down to the silver scar above the left eye.' Charlie Grant paused briefly, then went on, 'Next point, there was one sailing by the MacQuaid Shipping line yesterday afternoon,' he said, 'and that was out of Greenock bound for British Guiana. According to the passenger manifest, there were five single men on board, though none by the name of Christopher Hadden.'

'There is no reason why he should be travelling on a MacQuaid ship, or even under his own name for that matter. If he plans to set up an entirely new life for himself he might as well start now.' Jarrett shrugged lightly. 'Anyway, this is all entirely hypothetical. The chances are he is still right here in the city.'

'I would agree with that. He is unlikely to walk out on his sister without giving her some

48

idea of what was happening.'

'Why not? We don't know anything about their relationship. He may very well hate her with a passion.' Jarrett let this sink in briefly, then, 'Or she might not be as ignorant of the robbery as she would like us to think.'

Charlie Grant looked thoroughly disapproving of this suggestion.

'I find that most difficult to believe, Superintendent,' he said. 'It's not really the sort of crime respectable women get involved in. Helping unwanted husbands to pop off, or running a high-class house of questionable purpose, but tunnelling into a bank — '

'I am not suggesting she actually swung the pick, Inspector Grant, but nobody would have been in a better position to arrange everything, even to the extent of evicting the upstairs' occupant so that the gang would not be overheard.'

'Perhaps someone should talk to her again.'

'I have every intention of doing so. In fact, I have a warrant to search her brother's room, so I'll sound her out a bit more. Who can say what she might let slip?' Jarrett then consulted his list of immediate tasks. 'You had better take over the enquiries at the Woodside Coal and Shale Company, along with Detective Constables Williamson and Russell. Even if you cannot identify possible suspects, you might try to get some idea of how long it would take to create a tunnel of those dimensions. Indeed, any information would be helpful.'

Charlie Grant nodded, but there was more on his mind.

'I know you're concerned about this arsenic report, Superintendent,' he said, 'but do you really think that the Chief Constable would consider asking for an exhumation order?'

'He was in a reasonable mood when I left him yesterday,' Jarrett replied. 'Being able to name Christopher Hadden and the prospect of running him to ground, not to mention the possibility of his cohorts being among the Woodside workforce, cheered him up as much as anything short of the promise of a knighthood might do.'

'Yes, but the Western Bank affair is his primary concern right now. It's his kind of people who have been targeted. If we start talking about Jacob French and Alexander Bisley he is naturally going to assume that we are being less than single-minded about this.'

'So are you suggesting that we ignore the possibility that Alexander Bisley murdered his uncle?'

'No, sir, I am suggesting that it might be a better idea to get the Western Bank matter firmly in the bag, then take advantage of Chief Constable Rattray's good humour to pursue the possibility of an exhumation.'

'You might be right,' Jarrett said solemnly, 'but I can't help feeling that Bisley's mother is at serious risk. If he did kill his uncle, she is next in line.'

'But it might take some time for the will to be settled on her.'

'Why should he wait until settlement? Seraphina Bisley might depart this world at any time, and I would hate to think that I had done nothing to prevent it.'

'Is she of an age?'

'We are all of an age, Inspector. What I do not know is whether she has any medical condition that might mask a criminal act.' Jarrett shook his head grimly. 'Trouble is, I am not quite sure how to find out without alerting Alexander Bisley.'

'Very tricky, sir,' Grant agreed. 'Especially as there's always the possibility that your Mr McConnell could be entirely mistaken and the only real murder victims were rats.'

'There is that to be considered, but I don't really believe it. I think the body of Jacob French should be examined, but perhaps we should let Dr Hamilton advise us on this one. He can do the Marsh arsenic test, so he will be able to tell us if a delay would be detrimental to the investigation.'

'That being so, Superintendent, an opportunity presents itself.'

'The Megan Speirs business, you mean?'

'To put it as delicately as possibly, sir, Dr Hamilton is due to confirm the girl's claim this afternoon. We could get an immediate answer to the question of disturbing the ghost of Jacob French.'

'Very well,' Henry Jarrett agreed, 'but everything has to be juggled, because as you very well know, Inspector, we are short of experienced senior officers.'

⋆　⋆　⋆

Tommy Quinn had his own demons. They came unannounced when he let his guard down and took the form of soundless glimpses into the long past. It was a time before he crossed the sea, before his youth, even before school. Although unwelcome, they served to remind him of who he was and why he did what he did.

His mother always favoured the same flat, flower-carpeted spot by the stream for their summer picnics. It was only her and him, of course, because his solicitor father had been rubbing shoulders with the Dublin Anglicans for so long that he had come to regard all pleasure as sinful. Indeed, that one day each week was their break from the quiet, proper world of the new sedate, middle-class suburbia.

Then came the blight. It was black against the sun, and carried a sickle that glinted here and there along its lethal, curved blade. It may have been because of this thing that there was no violence, or it may have been that she believed that by staying calm the boy would also remain calm. Even without knowing the precise circumstances, that was how she would be. Her first thoughts were never for herself.

Across the span of years he saw again the contorted mask of the blight and his mother's bouncing ringlets. And her eyes, wide and unblinking, staring at him but not seeing. It was a look of utter disbelief, because the unthinkable had come to visit her.

Inspector Grant might see this as just another case, but to Sergeant Quinn it was much more than that. He didn't want to take it on, because like any other normal male it made him uncomfortable. But now that fate had foisted it on him he intended to see it through. Although he would never say as much to Jarrett and Grant, catching this animal now meant much more to him than recovering the precious property of the immorally wealthy, most of whom were borderline criminals in their own way. Why else would one need an undisclosed safe deposit box?

Grace Martin's folder was as thin as a beggar's belly. A housemaid of sixteen summers, accosted on the evening of her fortnightly day off while returning home, she wisely offered no resistance when threatened with the blade and was indecently assaulted and ravished. In other words, a facsimile of the Megan Speirs offence.

Sergeant Quinn's main concern was that sooner or later one of the victims was going to fight back, and when that happened he might well have a corpse on his hands.

★ ★ ★

He had been lounging in his usual spot for so long he had almost become invisible, no more deserving of a second glance than any other fitting on the grey wall. In a sense, that was his real strength. The fewer people who knew Vincent Gittens by sight the better.

It wasn't easy to impress the *Advertiser's* cast-iron editor, Jake McGovern, but Gittens intended to do so. Although he had only come to Glasgow from the *Paisley Courant* a few months earlier, his ruthlessness and tenacity had already earned him the jealousy and dislike of the rest of the staff. But he was used to that sort of thing and it didn't bother him. In his world, the price of a drink was an investment that always paid high dividends.

During one of the rare lulls in activity in the main hall at Glasgow Central, Gittens pushed himself away from the wall and glided over to Desk Sergeant Davie Black.

'Got a bit of something for me, Davie?' he asked softly, tucking a half crown under the ledger. 'There's a good few pints for you.'

Davie grinned.

'Quiet time, Vince?'

'Sadly, yes. There hasn't even been a bloody hanging for God knows how long.'

'Oh, I'm sure we can find someone to hang if that's what you want. After all, you're not too particular.'

Gittens shook his head, grinning.

'Don't be like that, Davie,' he said. 'We all have to earn a crust. Take you lot, for instance. You're nothing but glorified rat catchers.'

Davie Black considered this and had to concede it.

'Never really looked at it that way,' he admitted, 'but I suppose you're right.'

'Of course I am, so how about something tasty?'

'You know about the bank?'

'Not everything. Your investigation department is being very cagey about the whole thing. All any of us have got is a snippet or two from the doorman at the Western Bank, and he didn't know hellish much.'

Davie Black selected one of his precious sheets of foolscap paper, quartered it and tore it into four. He scribbled a few relevant details and slid it over to the newspaperman.

'A suspect,' he said. 'So far the only one.'

Gittens's eyebrows shot up.

'Have they brought him in?'

'They can't even find the bugger.'

'Excellent, excellent. Good chance here to pip them at the post.' Gittens grinned broadly. 'Any other little morsels? Be worth a pint or two.'

'What about a ravishing?'

'Now that could be a nice little extra. McGovern is fond of a bit of colour, something that will give the old maids their jollies. Nothing sells papers like extreme naughtiness.'

Davie Black took the scrap of paper and added a few details before skimming it back.

'Don't say I'm not good to you,' he said.

'Much obliged to you, my friend. I'll remember you in my will.'

'Don't bother. I don't need another broken pencil.'

If Mrs Stuart was surprised to see Henry Jarrett again, and so soon, she certainly didn't show it. In fact, the superintendent was already of the opinion that very little could cause her inscrutable expression to change. Perhaps enduring the loss of both parents to fever in India and having to forgo the pleasures of childhood at an early age had made her tough and resilient.

'Christopher would never flee the country like a common crook,' she stated after the maid had left the room and drawn the doors behind her.

'It is only a theory, Mrs Stuart,' Jarrett said. 'We believe he may have arranged everything so that he could catch the train to Greenock immediately after the robbery, and there board the *Constellation* for Georgetown.'

'Never.' Mrs Stuart invited him to sit on the far side of the low table, despite his protestations yet again that he only took Black Dragon tea, and then only if properly infused. The stalemate had been breached by the maid being told to bring coffee, although even here he had his clear and distinct favourites. But he did want very much to examine Christopher Hadden's room, so he would yield a little. When he was settled Mrs

Stuart added, 'You don't know Christopher, Superintendent Jarrett. I have no doubt that your profession leads you down the path of cynicism, and I can well understand why, but not everyone is weak and criminal by nature. My brother would not steal, even if his very life depended upon it.'

'Mrs Stuart,' Jarrett pointed out, 'we have positively identified Mr Hadden as the man seen in the shop doorway on two consecutive evenings, and who also rented the shop and the house above from Hillyard and Palmer, giving his name as Benjamin Laird. Now, if you know anything that would explain your brother's interest in a property used by bank robbers, or tell me where he is, we could at the very least exclude him from our enquiries.'

'How could I possibly know about this robbery?' Mrs Stuart asked, but kept her composure and fell short of demanding. 'Are you suggesting that I was somehow involved in a crime, and furthermore aided my brother's disappearance?'

'Mrs Stuart, I am not suggesting anything. I am trying to make sense out of disparate facts, and the only thing we are certain about is Christopher Hadden's involvement in the crime.' Henry Jarrett let this sink in, but the delay also gave him time to collect his thoughts. He may have been bordering on the aggressive, which only seemed to harden Mrs Stuart's resolve, so perhaps it was time to give her a way out. 'It is possible, Madam, that Christopher was somehow coerced into participating in something which you maintain is contrary to his nature. That sort of thing is not at all unusual. He may have been threatened, or indeed the gang may have threatened you. He would not have told you about that for fear of scaring you. Then again, it may have been blackmail.'

'Blackmail?' Mrs Stuart leapt on the word. 'What on earth could anyone find to use against Christopher?'

'I can't possibly imagine. Something to do with his military service, perhaps?'

'Unthinkable. Christopher was a captain in the Royal Engineers.'

'In that case, he may have been threatened by a disgruntled soldier.' Even as he said this, Jarrett knew how foolish it must have sounded, yet Mrs Stuart was obviously willing to accept any explanation that did not involve her brother's culpability. 'Now, I would like to see Mr Hadden's room, Madam, if that is all right with you.'

The lady of the house had no intention of allowing Henry Jarrett to rummage at will through Christopher's belongings without being present and observing everything. Accordingly, she led the way up the broad staircase to a door-lined hall and, after pausing briefly, turned the large brass knob and sailed into the room. It was as though she was either fearful of what she might find, or was unused to encroaching on Christopher's private domain.

'This is my brother's private room,' she said, 'but of course the entire house is at his disposal, my boudoir excepted. We must each have somewhere that is entirely our own, don't you think?'

Jarrett could scarcely agree more. His own room, with its large Wardian case containing a nice selection of ferns, was his private place after a busy day. It was somewhere to escape to, somewhere in which to think calmly without interruption, and that process of closing the door on the greater world was more than just a mechanical act. It was a necessary ritual. The click as the steel tongue sprang into its keeper echoed and re-echoed in his mind for some seconds, while a great peace seemed to flood his whole being and he just revelled in his escape from the outside chatter and madness of it all.

'Do you have the key to Mr Hadden's bureau, Mrs Stuart?' the superintendent asked.

'Certainly not. Christopher's business is entirely his own affair.'

Jarrett nodded. Strange woman, he thought. Or lying. More than likely lying.

He found the small, bronze-coloured key in a crystal bowl on the mantelpiece and quickly slid up the roll-top to reveal a neat array of pigeon holes, drawers and a writing slide with an adjustable slope. The ink, dipping pens and the rest of the paraphernalia were nicely secured in holders and racks.

The ease with which Jarrett found the key told him that there would be nothing of immediate consequence within the figured walnut Davenport. By that he meant there would be no obvious links to the robbery at the Western Bank. Whatever else Christopher Hadden may have been, he was no fool.

As anticipated, the bureau contained nothing of real interest, so Jarrett turned his attention to the chest of drawers which stood against the opposite wall. Once again, there was nothing that might be deemed incriminating, although beneath the folded long Johns there was a small selection of gentleman's art, in which slightly overweight ladies with wisps of semi-transparent gauze failed utterly to make themselves decent. At least that eliminated one area of operations that invited blackmail.

Not that Jarrett had for a single moment believed his own fiction. The idea that Hadden might have been pressured into breaking the law was purely an escape route for Mrs Stuart, a glimmer of light at the far end of an otherwise dark tunnel that just might provide her with the opportunity to speak out of turn. The lady, however, did not respond as he had hoped. Instead, she mainly kept her own counsel as she watched him move around the large room, checking this cupboard and that closet, closely examining each and every item, but always replacing everything precisely as he had found it. Only when he moved the high-backed wing chair aside and lifted the corner of the floral Templeton carpet did Mrs Stuart's patience reach its limit.

'Superintendent Jarrett,' she said forcibly, 'I really must know whether you are looking for something specific, or merely hoping to uncover some flimsy scrap of doubtful evidence.'

By way of an answer, Jarrett retrieved a sheet of coarse paper from beneath the thick underfelt, considered it for a few moments, then held it out for her to take.

'The dimensions of a tunnel, Madam,' he said flatly. 'Forty-two feet in length, three feet in width and three feet in height. Coinciden-tally or otherwise, these are the exact measurements of the tunnel used by the gang who robbed the Western Bank.'

For a full half minute Mrs Stuart could not bring herself to speak, then somehow managed to recover her self-control and said, 'This is not Christopher's writing. Someone clearly wishes him harm.'

'Who would want to do that, Mrs Stuart?' Jarrett replied. 'And perhaps you would like to tell me how this mysterious individual gained access to your brother's room? I find it quite impossible to imagine how a stranger could enter this house without being admitted by the maid or seen by you.'

Mrs Stuart shook her head as she sought the right words. She was still outwardly calm, but inwardly she was in turmoil.

'There was someone here,' she said quickly. 'I don't know his name.'

'When?'

'About a week ago. Christopher rarely entertains, but he did have a guest on that occasion.'

'You must have met him. What did he look like?'

'I was introduced to the man, yes, but I hardly said a dozen words to him. He was of medium height, swarthy and quite thin.'

Jarrett retrieved the sketch, folded it carefully and tucked it away in his coat pocket. He was far from convinced by Mrs Stuart's story, which sounded for all the world like a desperate explanation, concocted in panic. Yet somehow he knew that she would stick to that story whatever he said.

'Thank you for cooperating, Mrs Stuart,' Jarrett said. 'But I should warn you that I may be back with uniformed officers to search the entire house.'

4

It was baked stuffed rabbit for dinner. Mrs Maitland placed the animal in a large basin of cold salted water to clean it well, then left the kitchen to the girls while she went off to write a letter of condolence to her old friend, Daisy Sinclair, whose father had finally shrugged off these mortal coils after threatening to do so on numerous occasions. It went without saying that she would have to visit her in Pollockshaws, but that was a bit of a tiresome journey by horse-bus, especially as it tended to get caught up in a log jam every few minutes. Also, although she hated to admit it, she never felt entirely easy about leaving the maids in charge of her beloved house. She had toyed with the idea of inviting Daisy to call upon her, but that seemed singularly inappropriate in the case of a death. No, sooner or later she would have to go to Daisy.

There was no question of her going to the old man's funeral, of course. That would have been unthinkable. He was of the old school, so there would be no immediately connected women at the graveside. Not even his wife, had she still been alive, or his daughter, or indeed any female relative or family friend. Traditionally, the only female permitted to attend the internment would be his mistress, since this would be her only chance to say farewell. That way, the entire matter was taken out of the hands of possibly vengeful females and made into an accepted part of the ceremony. Furthermore, it meant that any woman joining the mourners was what she was and there was no need to proclaim it.

For once, Lizzie Gill was being entrusted with the stuffing. Elsie Maitland didn't give her a reason for this, but it was probably because she felt that the time was right. Jeannie Craig was new to the household, but Lizzie had come as a child of twelve years and was now seventeen, so the lady of the house was not exactly rushing her into new responsibilities.

Yet that was precisely how Lizzie felt. It was a great demonstration of faith and for someone who was as naturally apprehensive as she was, so much could go wrong.

'There's nothing to it,' Jeannie said, laughing. 'I'll help you with the bread-crumbs.'

'That's the least of my worries.' Lizzie chewed her lower lip as she read and re-read her scribbled note. 'They're used to things always being exactly the same. That's the trouble with the paying guests. They don't like change.'

'Why should they notice? There's only a couple of things in it.'

'No, there isn't. Breadcrumbs, suet, parsley, onion, mixed herbs, an egg and seasoning. And another egg to brush all over the stuffing balls when I've made them.'

'All right, I'll chop the onion for you as well.'

'You don't chop it, silly, you have to mince it. See what I mean about it turning out different? If you gave them chopped onion in their stuffing balls they'd riot. I'm sure of it.'

'Listen, if Mrs Maitland thought you'd make a mess of it she wouldn't let you anywhere near it.' Jeannie continued to grin as she diced the carrots. More often than not, the vegetables had to be chunky, but this time Mrs Maitland wanted the carrots and turnips mashed, which meant cutting them all to the one size so that they would be ready together. 'Anyway, Sweetman is away and Croall is probably going to be late again, so that only leaves Jarrett and McConnell. You're getting off lightly, if you ask me.'

'Well, I'm not too sure of that.' Lizzie glared at her across the large, well-scrubbed kitchen table. 'And it is Mr Jarrett and Mr

McConnell to us.'

Jeannie made a face.

'All right,' she said, but took it in good part. Although Lizzie had not been designated her superior, nevertheless that was precisely what she was. It was all a question of sensing rank without having it imposed upon her. 'Do you know, if Mr McConnell would go to the theatre or something they could get to it.'

'Who?' Lizzie asked, confused. 'Get to what?'

'Oh, don't act daft, Lizzie Gill. I'm talking about Mrs Maitland and the superintendent.'

'Why, you dirty little devil!' Lizzie started to giggle then, and when she began there was nothing for it but to let her run out of steam. 'What on earth made you say that?'

'This and that. I mean, you never know what you're going to come across, do you?'

'Unless you go looking for it you won't come across anything in this house, Miss Craig.'

'Then why are you still giggling? It's because you know more than you're letting on, isn't it? I've only been here a few weeks yet I know what I know. You've been here since Moses was a wee boy, so you must have seen everything.'

'I certainly have not!'

'Liar. If you tell me what you've really seen, I'll tell you.'

'Don't be silly. I think this has gone on far enough.'

'Suit yourself.' Jeannie adopted her annoying couldn't-care-less face, and tried hard to give the impression that producing precisely cubed root vegetables was at least interesting, if not downright absorbing. 'We'll say no more.'

'Good.' Lizzie somehow managed to control herself by deliberately not glancing in Jeannie's direction. One look at that fake picture of intense concentration would have set her off again. In the end, however, her curiosity got the better of her and she asked, 'Have you been looking through keyholes?'

'Only one keyhole,' Jeannie admitted, 'and it wasn't yours.'

'You wouldn't have learned much if it had been. So whose was it?'

'You know whose it was.'

'And?'

'Let's just say it's no more or less than you'd expect, all things considered. She's no age for a widow, after all, and she's not one of those who settles into wearing black for the rest of their lives. That's not the sort of keep-out notice she cares to give.'

Lizzie shrugged lightly.

'I'm not sure I believe you,' she said. 'She was in service too, you know, so there's nothing she doesn't know about maids' funny little ways. For one thing, I can't see her being caught in front of a keyhole.'

Jeannie's mock concentration failed her then and she made a face that conceded partial defeat.

'Well, not actually caught,' she admitted, 'but nearly, if you know what I mean.'

'My God, you're infuriating,' Lizzie said. 'You really drive a person to the very brink, don't you?'

'That's only because you want to know just as much as I do. You'd be a bit odd if you didn't.'

★ ★ ★

Superintendent Jarrett and Sergeant Quinn arrived more or less simultaneously at Dr Hamilton's oak-panelled hallway in his Porter Square residence, which nestled very neatly behind the new Sheriff Court and its adjacent City Mortuary.

Charlie Grant had not yet returned from his sojourn to the Woodside Coal and Shale Company's site on the Paisley Road, and it was by no means certain that he would have advanced their hunt for the actual diggers,

70

but either way Henry Jarrett was temporarily in a state of limbo. He could pursue the question of arsenical poisoning without feeling that he was stealing time from other, more pressing matters.

They had only been waiting for five minutes or so when Dr Hamilton appeared at the door of his surgery and was temporarily joined by the girl, Megan Speirs, and her omnipresent employer, Miss Emily Monk. Although both were familiar with Tommy Quinn, neither acknowledged him as they glided past on their way to the outer world and Miss Monk's waiting carriage. This most unnatural consideration for a servant was not lost on the detectives, but it was allowed to pass without comment. That would not have been the case had Inspector Grant been present.

'I understand that you are taking to do with this case, Sergeant Quinn,' Hamilton said when the females were well out of earshot. 'I will send you my report, but it is really an unsurprising state of affairs. The girl was accosted and penetrated at knife-point. There is no real evidence of forcible entry, and she was not a virgin when the attack occurred, which no doubt weakens your case somewhat.'

'Am I right in assuming that the same

character assaulted Grace Martin some three weeks ago?' Sergeant Quinn asked.

'I would go as far as saying probably, but there is nothing specific about either crime that could make me say that it was definitely the same man. Put another way, his words were few and indistinct, and he had no funny little perversions that would serve to link him positively to Grace Martin and Megan Speirs.'

'But it is reasonably certain?'

'It is more than likely.' Dr Hamilton looked concerned. 'That is why it is all the more worrying.'

'I'm sorry?'

'Fewer than one in ten girls come forward to report such incidents, so what exactly are you up against out there, Sergeant? And for that matter, how long has this been going on? Had it not been for Miss Monk this is one more crime that would have gone unnoticed.'

This was exactly what Tommy Quinn had feared, and Dr Hamilton had now merely served to confirm it.

'If this character is a random attacker,' Quinn offered, 'we have very little chance of catching him, other than by a sheer fluke. But if there is any connection between the girls — '

'Then that's how to approach it,' Jarrett

stated. 'Forget the random element and look for some link, however tenuous. Unless the assailant either follows his intended victims until they reach some deserted spot, or is willing to loiter in a suitable place in the hope of a female chancing by, then there has to be a connection.'

'Following is a possibility, Superintendent,' the sergeant said, 'but loitering would be too risky. Sooner or later he is going to be spotted, if not by the officer on the beat, then perhaps by a conscientious citizen. No, I think we should rule that out.'

'In that case, might I suggest that you talk to both girls and try to find some common factor. Perhaps they are members of the same association, or visit a church group or theatre on their time off.'

When Tommy Quinn had hurried off with fresh hope and more optimism than he was really entitled to muster up, Dr Hamilton said, 'I understand you want to see me on a different matter, Superintendent.'

'Indeed I do. It's about arsenic.'

'Really?' Dr Hamilton was immediately interested. 'Please go on.'

'Well, to cut a long story short, I have been given information concerning the purchase of an inordinate quantity of the poison.'

'And you think it is going to be used for

nefarious purposes?'

'I think it has been.' Jarrett let this sink in. 'Have you heard of Jacob French?'

'The hotelier? Yes, I met Mr French on a couple of occasions, but I had no dealings with him professionally.'

'His funeral was last Friday.'

'So I believe.' Dr Hamilton smiled wickedly as he peered into Jarrett's eyes. 'My God, you don't think that the old devil was helped along to perdition, do you?'

'I think it may be a strong possibility.'

'Then you have to tell me everything you know. French was a well-known individual, so it makes it all the more interesting that he should have been despatched.'

'May have been despatched,' Jarrett corrected. 'At this moment of time all I have to go on is the fact that a member of his family bought more arsenic than might be thought proper for the elimination of rats.'

'How much?'

'A three shilling packet.'

'Sounds like murder,' Dr Hamilton said. 'That's twice as much as Madeleine Smith used to get rid of L'Angelier.'

'So you think she was guilty?'

'As sin, Superintendent, but no jury was going to send a young middle-class lady to the gallows.'

74

'This particular party doesn't have that to rely upon.'

'Might I ask the name of the suspected person?'

'Alexander Bisley.'

'Dr Hamilton's eyes widened.'

'The nephew? Good God, man.'

'You know him?'

'I certainly do. An ambitious young fellow, but pleasant enough and the last person I would have thought capable of killing his uncle.'

'Everybody is capable of killing his uncle, Dr Hamilton, as you very well know. In this instance, however, it is not Jacob French's fate that concerns me.'

'Sorry?'

'The estate, hotel and every penny he had goes to his sister, Seraphina Bisley, Alexander's mother.'

'And you think he would kill his own mother for this inheritance?'

'I have known them to do it for a great deal less.' Jarrett eyed the police surgeon quizzically. 'You will keep this to yourself, Dr Hamilton?'

'Of course. It is not exactly the code, but I can see how you might not want it made public until you pounce.'

Jarrett laughed then.

'Is that what I do,' he asked, 'pounce?'

'You know what I mean.' Dr Hamilton's long face instantly assumed its normal dour expression. 'It's going to be a fight, Superintendent. I am my own man, and I believe you are too, but to achieve what I think you have in mind would necessitate the Chief Constable putting in a formal request. For reasons I don't particularly want to go into, that is not likely to happen.'

'They can't refuse an exhumation.'

'Oh yes they can, unless you have evidence that is so damning it would endanger their very careers. My advice to you, Superintendent, is to tread carefully and bide your time.'

'But isn't time a factor? Would you still be able to carry out the necessary test after, say, several weeks or months?'

'I would be able to perform the Marsh test a generation from now. That is the greatest risk an arsenic murderer faces, you see. The victim dies but the traces never do.'

If not exactly elated, at least Henry Jarrett felt that all was not lost as he took his leave of Dr Hamilton and rejoined PC Jamieson on the Wagonette. As Domino trotted them out of Porter Square, the superintendent had cause to feel reasonably pleased with the situation, even though his concern over Mrs Bisley's safety still remained.

Inspector Grant's return to the office was marked by a considerable amount of patting and brushing of his coat.

'I'm going to need a tub tonight, sir,' he announced.

'I only asked you to make enquiries,' Jarrett said, 'not join in.'

'You don't have to go down the pit to get like this. All you have to do is walk around the yard.'

'And where did all this walking around the yard get you?'

'Almost nowhere.' Charlie Grant settled down in a cane chair and made a big thing out of lifting first one booted foot, then the other, because even a few seconds in the air provided great relief from the incessant pounding of heavy leather soles on ironstone cobbles. 'They have over three hundred miners underground and nearly twice as many surface workers.'

'In shifts, of course.'

'Yes, but it doesn't help, Superintendent. The plain truth is that we will not be able to identify the diggers, even if they did come from the Woodside mine.'

'Reason being?'

'There would have been no need for them

77

to be absent from work. According to the pit manager, Mr Howell, three men taking turns at the face could dig a forty-foot tunnel through stony clay in ten or twelve hours. Put another way, the whole thing could have been completed in one long night. They didn't need all weekend.'

Henry Jarrett produced the sheet of paper he had found at Mrs Stuart's house and offered it to Grant.

'That is exactly what it says here.'

The inspector took it and immediately latched on to the scribble at the foot of the page.

'Does that say Port Seba?' he asked.

'Yes. It is on the Demerara River, a hundred miles south of Georgetown in British Guiana.'

'So Hadden did sail with the tide.'

'Or he wants us to think he did. This was left under the carpet where a reasonably astute investigator would find it. Had it been in his bureau it would have been too blatantly obvious but, on the other hand, he had to be sure it would be found. Also, Mrs Stuart, a quick thinker if ever there was one, referred to a visit by a 'swarthy' man to her brother. She didn't actually say 'foreign', but she knew that I would take it that way.'

'Which implicates her.'

'Not necessarily. I gave her a get-out opportunity, by suggesting that Christopher Hadden may have been coerced into breaking the law, and she jumped at it.' Jarrett retrieved the paper then and tucked it safely away in his waistcoat pocket. 'I am assuming that Hadden is still here. If not in Glasgow, then not too far away. But right now we need some proof of his involvement. If you notice, the gang already knew that they weren't going to encounter underground pipes or any other obstacles. Whoever organized this had access to the original building plans for that section of Byres Road. What we must now do is find out who has recently been consulting such drawings.'

'And where exactly might we do this, sir?'

'Start with the Town Hall in Argyle Street by the Tontine. Failing that, try the Lord Provost's office above the Court House in the Saltmarket. If neither of these places is used for the storage of building plans, perhaps they can tell you where to find them.'

★   ★   ★

The baked stuffed rabbit with mashed vegetables was followed by a blancmange of Irish moss, which Wilbur McConnell at first eyed suspiciously, then quickly grew to relish.

79

James Croall, however, had not managed to get back to Mrs Maitland's in time for the proper sitting, but he would not miss out over events that were not under his control. Elsie Maitland was firm but kindly, a combination Henry Jarrett found immensely attractive. Not to mention the fact that she did not require foundation garments to maintain an hourglass figure so desired by one sex and desirable to the other.

Jarrett, for his part, had probably eaten most things in his time in Hong Kong, and very early on in his career had learned not to ask. In his book, Elsie had excelled herself on this occasion. Always living up to her fine reputation as a professed cook for the gentry, that meant she could never be out of work, always had minions to do the skivvying and was treated with the utmost respect by one and all. The difference between professed and plain could scarcely be exaggerated.

For one thing, it ultimately led to her marrying the merchant, Ernest Maitland, a man enormously fond of his food and who seemed intent, from his first hour on earth, to eat himself to death. His good wife, however, tried her best to provide only wholesome, nourishing food, but he was determined to commit suicide by fork and eventually succeeded in this as he had in all of his pecuniary affairs. Now he lay in the Ramshorn Kirk yard, forever forty-five years of age, and proof of the power of appetite over common sense.

Which, bluntly put, suited Superintendent Henry Jarrett enormously. He had absolutely nothing against the late Mr Maitland, but his departure left Elsie in an extremely favourable way of things. Wisely deciding not to live on the capital, but instead to convert the house into a superior guest house for respectable single gentlemen, she thereby increased her lot. Even though she did not know it at the time, she had her heart set on someday marrying a senior police officer and retiring to a villa on the Clyde Coast. It was for this reason that all others were held firmly at bay.

When Jarrett rose to his feet, fully intending to relax in front of the Wardian fern case and contemplating the problems most requiring urgent attention, Elsie materialized at the dining room doorway, paused briefly to gather her thoughts and accept the fact that Mr McConnell had not quite finished. Although this meant that she could not speak openly, the matter was nevertheless sufficiently urgent to merit her gliding across the cherry-red carpet to come between Jarrett and the chemist in the far corner. She did not touch, of course, for that was the unspoken arrangement if others were present. And first names were also taboo.

'This is not going to please you,' she whispered. 'They have sent a constable to collect you. He is in the front parlour, and I believe Constable Jamieson and Domino are waiting for you outside.'

The first time Henry Jarrett laid eyes on Walter Chapman he had been a lanky youth who had just lost his job and had no prospects of finding another. It was on the superintendent's suggestion that the lad should apply for the constabulary, and he even encouraged Inspector Grant to second him. Now, just a few short weeks later, young Chapman had started to fill out and was even threatening to fill his uniform. Certainly, he carried himself with stiff-backed pride, although there was a slight suggestion of concern around his eyes because it was possible that Jarrett might not remember him. But that was entirely unnecessary.

'Good to see you again, PC Chapman,' the superintendent said warmly when he entered the parlour and found the lad standing like a beanpole, his helmet tucked under his arm in the regulation manner, badge burnished and forward. 'Like the force?'

'Best thing I ever did, sir.'

'And now you have a murder?'

'How did you know, sir?'

'Come on, lad.' Jarrett accepted his coat and hat from Elsie Maitland, who had got into the habit of fetching his outdoor apparel while at the same time not making an obvious fuss. 'They wouldn't send you at this time of night if someone had had their pockets picked. Unless it was royalty, of course.'

* * *

As ever, Charlie Grant and Tommy Quinn were waiting in the cobblestoned alleyway by the large sliding doors when PC Jamieson arrived at the former Turkey Red dyeworks and drew Domino to a halt.

'The CC is inside,' Inspector Grant advised quietly. 'Have you seen this, Superintendent?'

The *Advertiser* headline was bold and aggressive: BANK MOLES BAFFLE POLICE.

Jarrett read as much as he could take of it, then swept his hat from his head and nodded diplomatically to the uniformed officers who were positioned by the entrance to keep the great unwanted out. So far no one had turned up and hopefully nobody would.

Here and there within the deserted building clumps of wood wool and strawboard boxes broke the sheer empty nothingness of it. Even the large vats had been removed when the fabric printers had relocated to the Bleachfields.

'A complete bloody mess, Jarrett,' Rattray bawled. It echoed and re-echoed around the hollow building. 'You have seen what the papers are doing to us, I suppose? Where does this leave us now?'

Jarrett ignored this outburst and instead nodded to Dr Hamilton, whose private carriage sat behind Rattray's more elegant brougham by the kerb.

'He has been dead for at least twenty-four hours,' Dr Hamilton said flatly. 'It isn't pleasant.'

The body was naked and tied to a chair in the middle of the large, dusty expanse. The throat had been torn — rather than cut — from ear to ear and his chest hair was a mat of congealed blood. Jarrett walked slowly around the man, noting the way his wrists had been tied to the back legs of the chair, while his ankles were secured to the front ones. The head was slumped forward with the chin resting firmly on the chest, but even before Jarrett took hold of the man's hair and raised his face he knew what he was going to find. The thin silver scar above the left eye and the heavier, coarser wound on the shoulder identified him as well as any sign on his back might have done.

But it was the irregular chunk of cold wax encasing the victim's loins that made Jarrett shudder.

'Candle wax,' Dr Hamilton pointed out. 'He was tortured.'

Henry Jarrett got down on one knee and examined the knots that secured the limbs, but there was nothing about them that suggested a nautical connection. Nevertheless, they served their purpose admirably. When he again rose Rattray was glaring at him.

'I don't have to tell you how damned serious this is, Jarrett,' the CC growled. 'You gave me definite assurances and I in turn passed them on to certain interested parties. What do you think that makes me look like? How do you think I feel, letting down some of the most important men in the city?'

Jarrett came close to letting Rattray know exactly what he thought of his associates, but he wasn't quite ready to retire yet and somehow managed to keep control.

'I don't think anyone could have predicted this turn of events,' he said flatly, although within he was extremely angry at being loudly berated in front of junior officers. 'It doesn't make any sense.'

'Nothing about this crime seems to make

much sense. They burst open safe deposit boxes without knowing what they are going to find, and in the process damage important documents and cause a great deal of distress. Clearly they have no respect for their betters. You, Superintendent, are supposed to protect the great and the good from the riff-raff and you have singularly failed to do so.'

'It is almost impossible to prevent a planned crime without inside information,' Jarrett said, his fists balling. He was now in danger of going beyond mere dismissal. Striking a senior officer would mean a spell in Bridewell and the end of everything, and it was only the image of Elsie Maitland that held him back. 'However, I am confident that we can solve this one, sir.'

'Are you really? Well, I am not so sure. But just in case you require encouragement, I am giving you forty-eight hours to get this investigation back onto the right path, or I will remove you from the case and give it to Inspector Grant. He seems like a solid type, the sort working men might confide in.'

Jarrett stared at the Chief Constable's retreating shape until he had left the building and could be heard barking orders to his driver. Then the superintendent turned his attention on Charlie Grant, but before he could speak the inspector said, 'I didn't say a word, sir. Whatever the Chief Constable knows, it didn't come from me. Believe me, I don't yearn to be in charge.'

'I don't think he knows anything,' Tommy Quinn offered. 'It's just a bluff to scare us into action.'

'Not us, Sergeant,' Jarrett stated, 'me.'

'Do you think he means it?' asked Inspector Grant.

'Oh, he means it all right. The question is, what can we hope to achieve in two days now that the only lead has come to nothing?'

'If I may, Superintendent,' Dr Hamilton interceded, 'it might not have come entirely to nothing. There is always the nature of the wound.'

'Have you noticed something distinctive about it, Dr Hamilton?'

'I think so, but I need time to examine it more thoroughly. And this isn't the place.'

'Unfortunately, time is something we don't have a great deal of.'

'No, I heard the performance.' Dr Hamilton beckoned the waiting mortuary attendants forward and indicated that he wanted the remains transferred to the blood wagon. 'See me in the morning, Superintendent. I hope to have something for you by then.'

★ ★ ★

Elsie Maitland aside, Henry Jarrett's pride and joy was his Wardian plant case. Gothic in style, and as wide as the window recess, it stood waist high on an equally ornate iron stand. It served a dual role as haven for the various ferns which would otherwise have perished in the sulphuric acid-laden atmosphere of this, and indeed any, industrial city, and a source of great peace and relaxation for him after the pressures of the day.

Deep within that tiny green glade a small pool of water kept the atmosphere moist, while a little pottery fisherman on a stool seemed blissfully unaware of his complete failure to catch anything. On this particular occasion it too closely mirrored Henry Jarrett's own condition.

Behind this pool, ill-assorted lumps of mortar-caked brick did service as miniature scenery, while two taller examples served as cliffs, giving the whole scene a sense of scale. But the real occupants of the large leaded glass case were the ferns themselves — oak fern, soft shield, harts-tongue, venus's hair, maidenhair spleenwort, a tiny wall-rue and the superintendent's most recent acquisition, a cross-shaped lady fern, *Victoriae*.

As was his wont, when his thoughts required to be collated and clarified, Jarrett brought his cane chair close to the glass and let himself drift away from the here and now and into a timeless world of ferns and peace.

It was a world in which even Chief Constable Rattray could not get to him. Certainly, the Western Bank affair did take priority, but only because the city's most powerful men were demanding that it be so. But in his book, Hadden's murder, two assaults on young girls and the possible threat to Mrs Bisley were considerably more important and ought to have been properly addressed. Yet the protection of wealth has always taken precedence over human life and limb, so he had no right to be surprised at Rattray having boiled over and virtually lost control in front of the ranks.

Tommy Quinn would have to divide his time and efforts between hunting for the attacker and assisting in the bank investigation, but he was more than competent and that was well within his capabilities. If there was any link whatsoever between the girls he would find it. Both incidents occurred on a Monday evening, which may or may not turn out to have some bearing on the matter, but beyond that there was no immediate connection.

As far as Mrs Bisley was concerned, Henry Jarrett could not decide whether the dilemma he faced was real or imaginary. It was just possible that Alexander Bisley did require an excessive amount of arsenic to deal with a particularly severe plague of rats, but his uncle's demise, even though half-expected, was still uncomfortably coincidental. Also, the quantity purchased would undoubtedly serve for at least two murders. In Bisley's favour, however, was the fact that he openly purchased the poison from Wilbur McConnell and signed the book fully and completely, making no attempt to falsify his name or address. In Madeleine Smith's case, detectives attempting to prove murder and disprove suicide or accidental death, had to scour the chemist shops throughout Glasgow before finally identifying three sixpenny purchases in her name and none at all in the name of L'Angelier. Inclined as he was to warn Mrs Bisley, Jarrett fully realized how that would sound to a doting mother and what it would almost certainly mean for his career. Anyway, it was by no means certain that she was not fully aware of the nature of her brother's departure, so that was yet another reason for approaching with caution, if at all.

Most pressing was the grisly fate of Christopher Jordan Hadden. Jarrett could well understand a falling out of thieves, because that was something he had encountered many times, but why torture the man?

The seemingly obvious answer was that he had secreted their ill-gotten gains, so the rest of the gang had to prise it out of him. Yet, the more he thought about it, the less he liked it. It sounded hollow and unreal. It was only money, so why endure that? Why not just tell them where it was and live to steal another day? And, for that matter, why did they rip open his throat as well as putting him through hell? Did any amount of treachery merit such treatment in a civilized land?

5

Generally speaking, communication at breakfast was limited to a nod of acknowledgement, but James Croall's reappearance at the window table suggested that things were returning to normal at the Western Bank and for that reason alone merited a few words. Wilbur McConnell, for his part, received a private assurance that his concerns over the arsenic purchases had not been forgotten, but it may take time to fully investigate the matter.

Having previously let Charlie Grant know that he would not be straight in at the usual time, Jarrett remained on the Menzies's horse-bus until it reached the Saltmarket, then proceeded on foot to the city mortuary where, hopefully, Dr Hamilton was waiting to give him his initial report.

'I gather you already have a name for this fellow,' Dr Hamilton said. He had turned the cotton sheet back to expose the throat wound. 'You will still require formal identification, of course. Going to be very unpleasant for someone. Known relatives?'

'A sister,' Jarrett said.

'Now that is too bad. Not the sort of thing I like to let the ladies see.'

'You don't know Mrs Stuart. Orphaned in India by the fever, became self-reliant at an early age, was subsequently widowed and now owns a considerable number of properties in the West End.'

Dr Hamilton frowned.

'Is this connected to the Byres Road bank robbery?' he asked.

'Just about as connected as it is possible to be. This is, or was, my one and only suspect. His sister owns the shop that was used in the tunnelling operation.'

'Good God, is she involved?'

'I am inclined to think not, but everything is still very much open to speculation.'

'And a source of contention, I dare say. Neither the Chief Constable nor your Inspector Grant was particularly forthcoming about this character, other than to say that he was known. That could mean anything.'

'The CC has not taken the loss of our only lead kindly,' Jarrett stated. 'But you were there. You heard it.'

'Indeed I did.' Dr Hamilton invited the superintendent closer and indicated a ragged tear that started beneath the left ear. 'The killer would have been standing behind him, pulling his head back by the hair and administering the death cut from left to right, if you could call it a cut. I am inclined against a blade of any sort.'

'Would you like to hazard a guess?'

'If I had to, I would suggest a large claw. A lion, perhaps, or a tiger. But of course other creatures are similarly armed. The crocodile, for example, or the bear.'

'But a single tear?'

'Not possible, I know. If it had been an animal his entire throat would have been torn out.'

'That apart, there is no trace of a creature at the death site.' Jarrett paused briefly. 'A claw attached to a handle would be my best bet. Something the killer could conceal about his person. It sounds like a symbolic artefact a witchdoctor might wave about.'

'There are not too many of them here either.'

Jarrett waited until Dr Hamilton had once more covered the face of the murdered man, then said, 'It might be better not to mention the wax to Mrs Stuart. She will have to know the cause of death, but I think we should leave it at that.'

'Agreed,' Dr Hamilton said, then asked, 'When do you want to bring her in?'

'Whatever would suit you best.'

'As soon as possible, if that is all right with you.'

'Very well, I'll pick her up in the wagonette after I have been to the office and made sure everyone knows what they are doing.'

★ ★ ★

Charlie Grant and Tommy Quinn had exhausted any news they may have had and were discussing developments in the American war when Henry Jarrett arrived and took his place behind the desk.

'Have you found any connection between the girls?' Jarrett asked.

'A very good one.' Sergeant Quinn beamed broadly as he placed a blue-tinted leaflet on the superintendent's blotter. 'They both attended the same improvement lectures on their day off.'

Jarrett lifted the flier and quickly scanned it.

'*PROFESSOR EUSEBIUS BECK, DISCOVERER OF ELECTRIC SALTS AND THE HEALTHGIVING EFFECT OF MAGNETIC LEVITATION. PRIVATE CONSULTATIONS BY APPOINTMENT.* And where exactly can we find this rogue?'

'The Corinthian Halls three evenings per week, Superintendent,' Quinn said. 'Otherwise Carling's Lodging House, Fiddlers Close off High Street.'

'Aptly named, Sergeant. What do you know about him?'

'Described by his assistant, Miss Amelia Moffat, and his female admirers as kindly, concerned and extremely trustworthy. By everyone else as a thieving, lying scoundrel and thoroughly lascivious.'

'Now that is interesting. Has his lasciviousness ever led him to the cells, by any chance?'

'Almost, but not quite, sir. Five years ago a case of indecent assault against him fell at the last furlong when the accuser failed to turn up. The actual charge was that he mesmerized women and took liberties.'

'What sort of liberties?'

'The limited variety. Professor Beck appears to be more curious than carnal.'

'Perhaps so.' Jarrett said, 'but he may have promoted himself. Better bring him in, Inspector Grant, and find out just what he has been up to.'

'Very good, Superintendent.'

'And while you are at it, Sergeant Quinn, perhaps you should talk to Miss Amelia Moffat.' Jarrett then turned back to Charlie Grant. 'Inspector, did you confirm that Hadden scrutinized the building plans for that block in Byres Road?'

'It was Hadden all right, sir. He spent some time in the County Clerk's office about a month or so ago. The archivist remembers him well, particularly because of the scar. Although it is all pretty immaterial now, the name he used was John Broadfoot. He said he was a speculative builder and needed to know if there had been any underground activity in the area.'

'There might be something in the name, but it is more likely that he simply pulled it out of the air. Just in case, however, it might be an idea to check the Glasgow Directory.' Henry Jarrett consulted his hunter and reminded himself that Dr Hamilton was waiting for Mrs Stuart's identification of the remains. As senior officer, he would also have to be present. 'Right now, I have to collect Hadden's sister and take her to the City Mortuary. Unless, of course, either of you would like to trade with me.'

They didn't, so each went about his appointed task, while upstairs Chief Constable Rattray tried to compose a letter of resignation which he hoped would not be accepted. Not that he had any real intention of submitting it to the Police Commission, of course. It was merely a gesture, nothing more. Nobody would dispute the fact that he was far too valuable to lose.

★ ★ ★

Professor Eusebius Beck was thin, angular and ageless. Had he stood erect he would probably have been slightly taller than average, but as it was he tended to give the impression of a slightly frail and somewhat pathetic individual. Inspector Grant was in no mood to be taken in by this act. Beck, he sensed instinctively, could run when he had to and probably did on numerous occasions.

'Am I under arrest?' Beck asked quietly once he was seated at the interrogation table. 'If so, I should like to know what I am being accused of.'

Grant considered one of several leaflets Tommy Quinn had found at the man's lodgings.

'Obtaining money by fraudulent means is one possibility,' he said.

'I am afraid I must object. You clearly have the wrong party.'

'Oh, I don't think so. Unless, of course, you can substantiate your claims.'

'Forgive me, but I really don't know what you mean.'

'Very well. '*Electric water distilled from a magnetic rock in the very heart of the Sahara Desert, and carried to civilization on swift dromedaries to rekindle youth in persons of great antiquity.*' Put another way, you are selling the secret of eternal life.'

Beck smiled thinly.

'You cannot prove it doesn't work,' he whispered.

'And you certainly can't prove that it does.' Grant stared at him for a few moments. 'Why aren't you twenty-one?'

'Pardon?'

'It's obvious, isn't it? If you possess such a secret the first person to benefit from it would be yourself.'

'Were I a selfish man, perhaps that would be correct, but I rarely think of myself.'

'You rarely think of anyone else. Tell me, Mr Beck, how does someone get to be such a complete and utter liar? Is it that you are incapable of telling fact from fantasy?'

'I object!' Eusebius Beck now sat bolt upright, his face a mask of indignation. 'You have no right to speak to me that way.'

'I've got every right. Anyone who gulls the defenceless and the bereaved is lawful prey himself in my book. Let me warn you, Mr Beck. If you can't persuade the judge of the validity of your claims you'll have plenty of time in Bridewell to think out your next piece of balderdash.' Grant leaned forward then and beckoned the trickster nearer. 'That, however, is not why you have been brought here. In fact, I would venture to suggest that your trickery is the least of it. What can you tell me about Grace Martin and Megan Speirs?'

Beck blinked at him as though he was talking a foreign language.

'I have absolutely no idea what you mean' he said.

'They attended your so-called improvement classes.'

'Many do. I rarely learn their names.'

'Unless they embark on a private consultation, no doubt.'

'Well, of course. The private consultation is a much more personal experience.'

'I dare say it is.' Charlie Grant shook his head. 'Quite something to remember.'

'What exactly are you suggesting, Inspector?'

'Let me refresh your memory, which clearly has not benefited from your '*ORIENTAL BRAIN ELIXIR, AS USED BY THE SAGES FOR CENTURIES.*' Five years ago you were detained on a charge of indecent assault.'

'I was found not guilty.'

'Not exactly. The case was dismissed when the lady in question withdrew her complaint and failed to put in an appearance.'

'Because she knew she was wrong.'

'No, because she knew she would be torn to shreds by the defence, who would proceed to wheel in half a dozen layabouts at a shilling a time to swear that they knew her well.' Charlie Grant consulted the original charge sheet. 'It says here that you interfered with her clothing.'

'Inspector,' Eusebius Beck said, his voice trembling with anger, 'if you knew the first thing about mesmerism you would know that to relax fully entails loosening tight garments.'

'Within reason.'

'If I may continue, the ladies today are so laced-up it is almost impossible for them to relax to any extent whatsoever.'

'I'll take your word for that,' Grant said. 'In the meantime, tell me where you were on Monday evening.'

'Forgive me. What does that have to do with anything?'

'Just tell me where you were.'

'At the Corinthian Halls, as I always am on Monday, Wednesday and Friday evenings.'

'Between when and when?'

'I arrive around six and the instruction class begins at seven. It lasts for one hour and if there are no private consultations I usually leave just after eight.'

'These times can be verified, I suppose?'

'Indeed they can. My assistant, Miss Moffat, is invariably there before I arrive and leaves with me when the janitor extinguishes the gas lights.'

Charlie Grant sat back and considered the man at length. According to Megan Speirs, the attack took place about five minutes after she left the horse-bus, but since she had no timepiece her best guess would place that about twenty to thirty minutes after the end of the lecture. Unless Miss Moffat was in some way involved, and that seemed totally inconceivable, it would not have been possible for Eusebius Beck to have followed the girl and carried out the assault.

It all depended on Sergeant Quinn's interrogation of Miss Moffat.

* * *

Amelia Moffat was probably somewhere in her late thirties, but since Tommy Quinn didn't ask and she didn't volunteer, that piece of totally irrelevant information remained unanswered.

'Tell me, Miss Moffat,' Quinn began, 'how long have you been associated with Eusebius Beck?'

'I have been Professor Beck's assistant for almost six years now,' She glared at him and silently dared him to refute a single word she said. 'I don't know what you think he has done, but I can assure you that he is a good and honest man who has helped many less fortunate than himself.'

'Less fortunate in what way?'

'Unable to cope with life's ups and downs. Professor Beck teaches them how to utilize the power of the self.'

'And what exactly do you do?'

'I play the piano and distribute the literature.'

'You play hymns and the like?'

'Oh, no. Professor Beck would never hear of it. He is not a religious teacher, Sergeant Quinn. In fact, quite the opposite.'

Tommy Quinn was mildly taken aback by this.

'What do you mean by the opposite?'

'I mean he teaches them to be at one with nature and how to commune with those who have crossed over.'

'Forgive me, Miss Moffat, but isn't that slightly contradictory? How can a non-religious person talk about Heaven?'

Amelia Moffat laughed then, but there was a sharp, derisory edge to it.

'That is so typical,' she said. 'Those who are under the thumb of the church cannot imagine natural survival of the being. Professor Beck believes that if you plant a seed in the ground it will grow, whether you dance around it with rattles and bells or just leave it alone. The strange costumes and mumbo-jumbo are inventions of the priest-men to reinforce their authority over the simple.'

'You may believe that if you wish, Miss Moffat,' Tommy Quinn said, finding it increasingly difficult to keep his temper, 'but we believe him to be a confidence trickster and worse.'

'What do you mean by worse?'

'I'll ask the questions, if you don't mind. Now, where was Eusebius Beck on Monday evening?'

'At the Corinthian Halls, of course.'

'Can you confirm his time of arrival and departure?'

'Yes, Professor Beck arrived at six o'clock. I had already been there for a good thirty minutes or so.'

'When did he leave?'

'Just after eight. We had no private consultations.'

'You saw him leave?'

'Naturally. We left together, Sergeant.'

'And went your different ways?'

'No, as always, Professor Beck escorted me to my lodgings in Bell Street, then went home.'

'As far as you know.'

'Where else would he go? He is a staunch

teetotaller, so the questionable attractions of taverns mean nothing to him.'

All that remained for Tommy Quinn was to compare notes with Inspector Grant, but as things stood, it did not look at all promising.

6

When PC Jamieson drew Domino to a halt in front of Mrs Stuart's residence in West Regent Street, Superintendent Jarrett assisted the lady down from the wagonette and followed her into the house. The aged retainer, for his part, quietly closed the large front door and disappeared in the direction of the kitchen. Once or twice there was the suggestion of a maid flitting from one room to another, but the household clearly ran like clockwork, effortlessly and without fuss. But particularly obvious by its absence was any sign or symbol of mourning.

Jarrett had been struck by Charlotte Stuart's serenity at the City Mortuary, but had put it down to her evident stoicism and self-control. The woman had seen much in her life and had already endured the loss of her parents and husband, at the very least, yet her utter impassiveness when identifying the corpse of her brother suggested indifference at best and callousness at worst.

'There never is a right time for this sort of thing, Mrs Stuart,' Jarrett said, 'but I would like to make a more thorough search of

Christopher's room. The important thing now is to find his killers.'

This time, she left him to get on with it and retired to find out exactly what had been happening to her household in her brief absence.

Jarrett had been supposed to find the paper beneath the carpet. Of that he was becoming more certain by the minute. Statistically, that part of the floor-covering immediately beneath the main armchair was most favoured by those who wanted to hide documents or paper money, but did not fully trust banks. Any detective worth his salt would know that and try it first. And that, of course, meant that the whole British Guiana factor had been designed to throw investigators off the trail. On the other hand, it may well have been a double bluff. Hadden might really have intended to flee to South America and made sure of not being trailed by leaving a clue so simple that a probationer could see through it.

But it was all entirely academic now. Whatever his real aims were, Christopher Hadden had not intended to get murdered. Above all else, that was the one thing Henry Jarrett could say with certainty. So what exactly went wrong and how did he wind up being tied to a chair, tortured and almost decapitated in a deserted factory by the docks?

This time the bureau came in for a complete and thorough examination. Nearby was a small table with a brass pot containing an aspidistra, that marvellous survivor so popular among those hopeless plant lovers whose care, or lack of it, was the kiss of death for almost every other piece of foliage. This he lifted and carefully placed on the floor below the window, so that all papers, envelopes and folds with broken seals could be lifted from the Davenport and piled up on a small mahogany stand. That allowed him to seek out the hidden drawer that almost certainly lurked within the layers of a false front or a double-bottomed drawer.

Jarrett first tried his pocket knife with the magnetized blade, skimming it over the sections of the drawers that might contain metal in the form of spring-loaded catches, but at no time did the steel encounter any resistance. He closed the knife and returned it to his coat pocket.

His next approach was to examine the rear or underside of each piece of wood by the Louis Braille method, at all times seeking that slight depression that will provide just enough of a hold to move a slide right or left, up or down. After ten minutes or so, he found just such an indentation on a wall of one of the pigeonholes, and was pleasantly surprised to discover that it slid forward an inch or so, before dropping free of its slats. Exposed was a thin wooden pocket containing a small blue envelope with a London postmark. There was no enclosure other than a small key, somewhat reminiscent of that which might be found in a lady's jewellery box. Jarrett tucked it into the fob pocket of his waistcoat and decided against mentioning it to Mrs Stuart. He then replaced the false segment of the pigeonhole and set about examining each document as he transferred it from the table to the bureau. There was really nothing of interest, but the bureau's contents were, if anything, neater than when he began.

Charlotte Stuart had just reached the foot of the stairs when Jarrett descended to take his leave.

'Barring some unforeseen development,' he told her, 'I don't think we will need to trouble you again, Mrs Stuart.'

'I am very pleased to hear that, Superintendent.' She gestured to the wizened retainer to come and attend to the door. 'I thank you for escorting me on that business, but wish from the bottom of my heart that it had not been necessary.'

'As do I, Madam.'

PC Jamieson was waiting quite contentedly on the driving seat of the wagonette and saluted the superintendent when he climbed on board.

'Back to Central, sir?' he asked cheerfully.

'Briefly, Constable.' Jarrett was clearly thoughtful and somewhat preoccupied. 'I will be wanting to go out again shortly.'

'I'll pass that on to Domino, sir.'

★ ★ ★

Jake McGovern owned and edited the *Advertiser,* so no one worked harder or came down more heavily on those who did not pull their weight. Right now, Vincent Gittens was the apple of his eye, but that could change very quickly and would do if Gittens failed to produce the goods. So far, however, the newspaperman had lived up to McGovern's expectations and justified the increase he was given when he left the *Paisley Courant.*

'Christopher Hadden,' Gittens said, perching himself on the edge of McGovern's desk. 'He was Jarrett's only real suspect and now he has been found dead.'

'Is that official?'

'Not in any way.'

'So just how trustworthy is it?'

'You can bet your salary on it.'

'No, Gittens, I'll bet yours on it.' If Jake McGovern had one ongoing ambition in life it was to be first with the news that mattered to the people of this city. At that very moment the temptation to splash Hadden's name across the front page of the *Advertiser* was very powerful, but with nothing more to go on than a source Gittens refused to divulge, he managed to resist it.

'Find out more about this man,' he said firmly. 'Background, family, everything.'

'Right away, Mr McGovern.' Gittens paused at the door before departing. 'What about the girl?'

'That always has potential. The reader likes a bit of scary titillation, but don't spend too long on it. The Western Bank fiasco is the big one.'

'So how much can I go, sir?'

'You can offer her a fiver but start with less.'

* * *

'Amelia Moffat and Eusebius Beck have provided each other with an alibi for the time in question,' Charlie Grant said when Superintendent Jarrett had taken his seat behind the desk. 'It is simply not possible for Beck to have been responsible for the attack on Megan Speirs.'

'What about the other incident?'

'Exactly the same situation. Their routine varies little.'

'Miss Moffat could be lying to protect him?'

'Indeed she could, sir,' Tommy Quinn put in, 'but there is no good reason why she should do such a thing.'

'Infatuation?'

'Clearly, that is a factor. Miss Moffat is a good and faithful assistant, but I really don't think she would be party to that sort of thing.'

'You have not yet encountered the full gamut of human behaviour, Sergeant,' Jarrett pointed out. 'I am not even sure that it is possible to do so.'

'I accept that, Superintendent, but I just know that they were telling the truth.'

'What about you, Inspector?' Jarrett asked Charlie Grant. 'Do you subscribe to this?'

'Reluctantly, yes. Much as I would like to put that charlatan away, it won't be for this. Unless, of course, he has some form of control over Miss Moffat, or Megan Speirs's guess of the time was well out.'

'But we already have Miss Emily Monk's statement, in which she gives the girl's time of arrival at the house. She was concerned because Miss Speirs was a few minutes late in returning from her fortnightly break and was studiously clock-watching.'

'Yes, that is one of the only two rock-solid facts in the entire affair.'

'And the other is?'

'The timetable issued by the horse-bus company. If Miss Speirs did not leave the vehicle when she says she did, then it would have to be half an hour earlier or later and that is impossible.'

'If you accept her story.'

'Sir?'

'Well, for one thing, we have no actual proof that she was at Beck's lecture. Neither he nor Miss Moffat remember her.'

'Are you suggesting that she might have been elsewhere?' Tommy Quinn said. 'Dancing, perhaps?'

'Do you find that difficult to accept, Sergeant?'

'No, but would she go alone? Young ladies tend to escort each other to such places.'

'Not always.' Jarrett toyed with the small key in his fob pocket and realized how much this Speirs matter was taking up valuable time. It was serious, certainly, but surely it did not need the attentions of three detectives? He was literally chewing at the bit to get on with finding Hadden's killer, while at the same time wondering how to obtain an exhumation order for Jacob French, and his patience with Tommy Quinn's solitary quest was running out. 'If she did go to the dancing alone and met some dubious individual, you have the whole world to choose from, Sergeant. But before you commit Williamson and Russell to a fruitless tour of these dens of iniquity, try to get the girl herself to sing a different tune.'

Henry Jarrett waited until Tommy Quinn had closed the door behind him and was proceeding along the corridor with a step made more lively by hope, then brought out the key and placed it in the middle of his blotter.

'First impression, Inspector,' he said.

Charlie Grant lifted the bright object, gave it a quick going over, then returned it to its spot.

'Jewellery box?' he offered. 'It isn't stout enough for a door or anything of that nature.'

'Agreed.'

'Do you mind if I ask where you found it, sir?'

'In a secret compartment in Christopher Hadden's writing bureau.'

'Do you think he found it in one of the safe deposit boxes?'

'Perhaps, but unless he knew what it was for it would be a useless acquisition, which is exactly how I feel about it.'

'There was no indication of its purpose?'

'Absolutely none. It was inside an envelope with a London postmark, but that might just have been a convenient pouch.'

'Nevertheless, it is worth considering.'

'Well, we might have to contact the Metropolitan eventually, although I fail to see what can be done with a postmark alone.' Jarrett lifted the key and offered it yet again to Charlie Grant. 'No fun, I know, Inspector, but I would like you to visit the banks on the off-chance that it is from a safe deposit box. You carry the authority young Quinn lacks. That could be important if they are all like MacPherson in Byres Road.'

'May I ask why Hadden should break into some safe deposit banks and rent another?'

'Just a wild notion. It occurred to me earlier that the best place to hide a precious object you have just stolen from a bank is in another bank.'

'So you think all that destruction was caused trying to find a specific object?'

'Inspector, I don't know what to think. It is only one possibility, but one that is worth eliminating before we go much further.'

Charlie Grant tucked the key safely away in an upper pocket of his floral waistcoat and gave it a pat.

'I suppose one slog is much the same as

another, Superintendent,' he said.

Then Tommy Quinn was back in Jarrett's office, having got no further than the telegraph booth at the end of the corridor before being halted in his tracks by the operator, PC Canning.

'Sorry to interrupt, sir,' he said, 'but we've got another one.'

'Another what, Sergeant?'

'A body, Superintendent. His throat's been cut.'

★ ★ ★

At least there was no sign of Chief Constable Rattray's chariot anywhere in the vicinity of the dockside warehouse.

'I understand the CC has a Lord Provost's dinner to attend this evening, sir,' Quinn volunteered as Jarrett, Grant and he stepped down from the wagonette. 'At least that is the word.'

'And you didn't think of passing that on?' Jarrett's annoyance was tempered by his relief at not having to put up with more verbal abuse.

'Sorry, Superintendent. I have a lot to think about.'

'Haven't we all? Anyway, that is of no real consequence. Just send for Dr Hamilton and let him know that we think it is another by the same hand.'

In truth, the only real similarity was in the fact that the victim's throat had been gashed open. Otherwise, the comparison was not really justified. This body was fully clothed and spread-eagled on the rutted flagstones, there was no obvious sign of torture and he had not been tied. It was only the relatively rare mode of killing that linked this crime to the murder of Christopher Hadden.

Dr Hamilton's presence was, if anything, a mere formality. The victim was evidently a man in his late thirties to early forties, approximately five feet seven inches tall and of stocky build. The palms of his hands were callused, but they were not the hands of a docker. No splinters or rope burns.

Jarrett then checked the jacket and trouser pockets and found nothing. Anything that might have identified the body had been taken.

'I don't think it was an attempt to make it look like robbery,' the superintendent said when he had finished. 'If you ask me, I would say that the killer or killers don't care one iota what we think. The removal of personal items was only to slow us down, but they know we will put a name to him sooner or later.'

Charlie Grant nodded his agreement.

'The hands, sir,' he said. 'Miner?'

'Very probably.'

'So this was one of Hadden's cohorts?'

'It would appear so.' Jarrett was confused and showed it. 'I was under the impression that Hadden had double-crossed the rest of the gang, who then squeezed out of him the whereabouts of their ill-gotten gains. I also assumed that they had then killed him, although I couldn't see why.'

'I know what you mean.' Inspector Grant lifted the man's cap, which was lying a few feet from the body, examined the inside for a name, then dropped it again when he found nothing. He grinned sheepishly. 'I suppose they would have thought of that.'

Henry Jarrett walked a little way away, then turned and surveyed the scene.

'Why here, Inspector?' he asked, neither expecting an answer nor getting one. 'What was a working miner doing in a dockside warehouse? But more to the point, why was he killed?'

'A further falling out of thieves?' Grant suggested. 'Or a duel for the loot?'

'Last man standing gets all?' Jarrett shook his head. 'I encountered that sort of thing in Hong Kong, but this doesn't seem to fit the bill.'

It was a full thirty minutes before Dr

Hamilton arrived, not overly pleased at having been dragged away from his practice to fulfill his obligations to the police commission. But he was nevertheless a civil man, who obligingly permitted the constable to accompany him in the carriage, when many another would have let him walk.

After Hamilton had made a preliminary examination, Jarrett asked, 'What about the time of death?'

'Sometime in the early hours of the morning, I would venture.'

'It would be as dark as the Earl of Hell's waistcoat,' Charlie Grant said. 'If the killers used a lamp the beat man would have spotted it.'

'Of course he would, but you paint an unlikely picture, Inspector. This man was killed elsewhere and dumped here. Nothing like enough blood. In fact, there is very little indeed.' Dr Hamilton looked first at the right palm, then at the left. 'You will have him down as a miner, I suppose?'

'That is what we thought.'

'Very well. I will go as far as declaring that he was a right-handed man, but whether he was a coal miner or stone worker will have to wait until I get him on the table.' Dr Hamilton rose from his kneeling position and made a few notes in his pad. 'By that I mean

I'll tell you once he has been under the knife. At his age I don't expect to find black lung, but there will be traces of whatever he worked with.'

Jarrett nodded appreciatively.

'Anything else?'

'I don't think so. Been through his pockets?'

'Nothing.'

'Quite as I would expect. If they took the trouble to bring him here by wagon they are hardly likely to leave you anything to go on.'

'Are you sure it was a wagon, Dr Hamilton?' Jarrett enquired. 'He might have been brought on a river craft.'

'I dare say it is possible, and it is worth considering, but all I can say for sure is that the settling of the blood, or lividity, shows that he lay on his left side for some time after death. I also think he was originally in a foetal position, which would be the case if it had been a wagonette, dog cart or some other vehicle with limited space.'

'That is a very good point, Dr Hamilton,' Superintendent Jarrett said, then added, 'Two people, would you say?'

'Yes, two. One taking the wrists, the other the ankles. No need for more than that and one alone would have found it difficult to manhandle a dead weight. Also, if he had been dumped by a single individual he would not be spread-eagled, just left to lie as and where he landed. Definitely two.'

★ ★ ★

Vincent Gittens was a past master of the art of waiting and watching. It was necessary in his job to develop a sniper's attitude to his prey, recognizing a powerful affinity to the still-hunters who supplied the Union Army in America with buffalo meat. They would silently and from a distance kill the big female who led the grazing herd, then wait until another natural leader emerged and kill her too. And so they proceeded, taking out one after another and piling up the bodies without ever causing a stampede. Lesser men would get too close, make a noise and lose them all in a sea of dust.

Gittens's lawful prey on this occasion was Megan Speirs. She had been beating a carpet in the rear yard of the house at Millburn Avenue when Sergeant Quinn arrived, and had reluctantly been given leave by Miss Monk to answer his questions. But rather than being possibly seen from the rear window of the other villas in relatively close proximity, she had suggested retiring to the dairy.

Quinn had remained there for just over fifteen minutes, asking questions and studiously entering the replies into his notebook. By the time he had finished, Vincent Gittens on the other side of the rubble and mortar wall knew everything he needed to know about the matter. The police had harboured doubts about certain aspects of the girl's story, but the young sergeant now seemed reasonably satisfied that she had in fact attended Beck's Improvement lecture at the Corinthian Halls, and that she had come straight home thereafter, barring one unplanned detour by way of the bushes with a knife at her throat. After consulting his watch, Tommy Quinn had brought the proceedings to a close and headed off for the horse-bus stance and presumably the police headquarters. Once he was well out of earshot, Gittens moved around the wall and silenced Megan with a hand over her mouth that was horribly reminiscent of her recent grim experience.

'It isn't what you think,' he growled softly. 'I'm from a paper with an offer of money.'

He let her struggling subside before taking a chance and removing his palm. But even then he was ready to pounce at the first indication of a hullabaloo setting up.

Megan turned slowly to face him. Although still unsure, she took heart from his inaction.

'Money?' she whispered.

'Yes, I am willing to pay you for your story.' Gittens opened a fist to reveal two sovereigns. 'How much do you earn, girl?'

'Twelve pounds for the year.'

'Well, there you are, two months' wages for a few minutes of your time.'

There could be no doubt that this small fortune was something she found difficult to refuse, but she was an uncomplicated girl, and as such feared being in the eyes of the world almost as much as the court of law.

'I can't spend gold,' she whispered. 'The bluebottles would have me for rifling some gent's pockets.'

'Mixed silver, then. Would that suit you?' Gittens made a fist, trapping the coins. 'You could say you saved it bit by bit.'

'Miss Monk would take it.'

'Not if she didn't know, but that's up to you. If you're daft enough to tell her maybe you don't deserve it anyway.'

For a mere second the girl's eyes flashed angrily, then she said, 'What do you want?'

Gittens shrugged lightly.

'Everything,' he said.

'Meaning?'

'What do you think it means? I can make the story up, so I don't need that.' Gittens was pleased with himself. Two pounds to the girl, three to himself and Jake McGovern gets a load of horse feathers. Not that he cared much about accuracy. He'd print it anyway if it tickled the old maids' fancy. 'Let's be honest, girl. It wasn't the first time the ferret chased the bunny.'

'It was still a crime.'

'I don't doubt it, but they won't get anyone. That detective just asks the same old questions because that's what he is paid to do.' Gittens tucked the sovereigns into his waistcoat pocket where they would keep the third one company. He had signed out three pounds in gold and two in assorted silver from Miss Ada Findlay in the front office, on the understanding that he would return that which was not required to secure the story. He dug into his coat pocket and brought out a leather money bag which he dangled in front of Megan's eyes. 'Two pounds' worth of half crowns, florins and a few shillings. Take you a while to put that together, wouldn't it?'

The girl's hand darted upwards to snatch the purse, but Gittens was unwilling to relinquish control of it just yet and drew it away sharply, cramming it back into his jacket pocket and grinning at her.

'It's mine,' Megan said softly. When he still refused to hand it over she breathed, 'Not here.'

'Then where?'

The answer remained unspoken as she stared past him at the dark figure gliding silently out of the inner hallway's deep shadows, its outstretched arm and scrawny, claw-like hand reaching for the nape of Gittens' neck. When he realized what was happening and spun on one heel to confront the veiled apparition, he was only inches from the flexing talons.

7

'First, the throat,' Dr Hamilton said warmly. 'Almost certainly the same claw device that was used to kill Christopher Hadden. I am still of the opinion that it is from a big cat and probably mounted on a handle, although whether it is ceremonial or merely functional remains to be seen. Whichever, the tearing nature of the wound is its signature.'

'African? Indian?'

'I really couldn't begin to guess. My instinct tells me that it must emanate from somewhere that large felines are found and perhaps revered. It makes no sense otherwise.'

Jarrett thought this over briefly.

'Have you determined whether this man was in a pit or a quarry?' he asked.

'This probably isn't what you wish to hear, Superintendent, but your man here has no coal or stone dust in his lungs. He wasn't a miner of the kind you imagined.'

'But his hands clearly show that he was.'

'They might just as easily be the hands of a navvy, or anyone else who wields a pick.' Hamilton turned back the cotton sheet and lifted the victim's left arm to let Jarrett see the tattoo clearly. 'Former soldier. 12th Company Royal Engineers. He was a sapper.'

'Good Lord.' Henry Jarrett looked closely at the Lion Rampant set against the St Andrews Cross, or Saltire. 'Christopher Hadden was a captain in the RE. Did he have a tattoo?'

'Officers rarely do, Superintendent.'

'No, of course.' This was a worrying turn of events and one that contradicted his most basic theories about the robbery. It made sense, albeit unpleasant, that Hadden could have double-crossed the gang and that they used brutality and torture to make him give up what they saw was rightfully theirs. But this new killing changed all that. In a peculiar way, Charlie Grant's suggestion that it might be a duel for the booty now made as much sense as anything else. Yet for some reason Jarrett still rejected it. 'What else can you tell me about him, Dr Hamilton?'

'Not a great deal. His most recent meal consisted of thin soup and coarse bread. There's no sign of meat, so my guess is that he was unemployed and probably relied on a soup kitchen. If he was married, the conditions must have been grim.'

Superintendent Jarrett crossed to the table on which the dead man's clothes had been laid out. If he was one of the discarded army of ex-soldiers, who were heroes in war and a nuisance in peace, the garments were probably given to him by a charity group, so tracing them to source would serve no useful purpose.

'Would you say these clothes were made for the man?' he asked.

'No. The jacket sleeves have been shortened, though not skilfully. The trousers are too wide and too short. The boots fit but I should imagine they were on the tight side.'

'That's more or less what I expected,' Jarrett admitted, and immediately dismissed the items from mind. 'What about habits, Dr Hamilton? Tobacco? Alcohol?'

'No evidence of either. Surprisingly for a man in his position, he does not seem to have sought oblivion. Even those with scarcely a crust to eat often manage to beg the price of a glass of cheap gin.'

'How very true.' The superintendent decided that there was nothing left to keep him here, and the City Mortuary was never his favourite place. 'Someone will be here shortly to take a collodion plate of this one. Is there anything you can do about the gash?'

'Don't worry, Superintendent. He'll have a scarf and look as good as he ever did.'

When Henry Jarrett left the coolness of the

City Mortuary and entered once more a bright, warm day in the world of the living, PC Jamieson quickly knocked out his pipe and snatched up the ribbons.

'Short visit that one, sir,' the driver said.

But the superintendent was in no mood for small talk. A very unpleasant thought had been tumbling around his mind for the last few minutes.

'Don't make observations, Jamieson,' he said, but there was no real admonition intended.

'Wouldn't do that, sir.'

'And don't always have the final word.'

'Wouldn't do that either, sir.'

★　★　★

Tommy Quinn flicked through the pages of his notebook until he reached his latest entries, such as they were.

'Megan Speirs has not deviated one whit from her original account, Superintendent,' he said in a tone that implied a measure of disappointment. 'Either she is telling the truth or she is a seasoned liar.'

'Hiding a liaison, you mean?'

'That is the only other possibility. She might have met up with someone and discovered that she was in for a row from

Miss Monk for being late home. The best excuse in a case like that would be one that elicited sympathy rather than a dose of the slipper, which is what she would have been given otherwise.' Sergeant Quinn gave a light shrug. 'I don't know, sir. It may have been a secret assignation, but I am inclined to believe her, particularly as she seems able to remember a fair amount of Beck's nonsense. I know that in itself is not absolute proof. Beck's lectures are always basically the same, so it is anything but conclusive.'

'Then what makes you believe her?'

'A certain conviction, which is rare in someone of her years. There is no sign of the lack of confidence usual in someone of that age. When she says something she means it.'

'That being the case,' Jarrett said, 'where do you go from here?'

'Much as I hate to admit it,' Tommy Quinn said, 'I have no idea. I really hoped that there would be some indication of who was responsible, but so far our only suspect turns out to have a better alibi than almost anyone else in the city.'

'Yes, convenient, isn't it?' Jarrett said. 'You know, Sergeant, I don't like water-tight alibis. Innocent people tend not to be able to prove beyond a shadow of a doubt where they were on a certain date. I know I couldn't, and I am fairly certain you couldn't either.'

Fast-approaching footsteps out in the corridor heralded the sudden opening of the office door and the arrival of Charlie Grant.

'I hope I'm not interrupting anything important,' the inspector said.

Henry Jarrett raised first one eyebrow, then both.

'You have something, Inspector Grant?'

'I do indeed. You were absolutely right, Superintendent. The key belongs to a box in the Northern and Overseas Bank in Hope Street.'

'Rented by?'

'James Waddell.' Charlie grinned broadly. 'The assistant manager, Mr Halliwell, describes Mr Waddell as a man in middle years, of average height and clean-shaven. In other words, fairly average, except for the thin scar above his left eye.'

'Excellent work, Inspector Grant. This more than makes up for my singular lack of progress.'

'And mine,' offered Tommy Quinn.

'So,' Jarrett went on, still beaming broadly, 'what was in it?'

'I have no idea.' Charlie Grant watched the expansive grin disappearing from the superintendent's face. 'They wouldn't let me open it. Didn't really believe I was who I said I was. If you ask me, sir, this Western Bank business has scared them all to buggery.'

'What do they want?'

'Probably yourself and a warrant.'

'Very well.' Jarrett rose from his comfy chair and reached for his coat. He had hoped that the next time he quit the office would be to make for home and Elsie Maitland's round of beef, with carrots, small greens and turnips. And it was his intention to drop in at Gowrie's Nursery behind the saw pit in Bell Square to pick a new fern for the Wardian case. So the sooner they got it over with the better. 'I will let the CC know that we need a warrant.'

★ ★ ★

If Findlay Botfield of the Northern and Overseas Bank wasn't related to Lawrence MacPherson he certainly ought to have been.

'As I explained to your assistant,' he said to Jarrett, much to Charlie Grant's annoyance, 'I have strict orders from headquarters regarding who I can and cannot admit to the rear departments.'

'I dare say you have.' The superintendent opened the double-fold that was the warrant Rattray had obtained at such short notice. It authorized him to examine the contents of one specific box. 'This also permits me to detain anyone who attempts to impede my investigation.'

No longer holding the winning hand, Botfield saved face by summoning his assistant, Mr Halliwell, and instructing him to give the superintendent and his assistant full assistance.

Once they were within the inner sanctum, Halliwell took the key, peered closely at the stamped numbers, then handed it back to Jarrett and retrieved the appropriate box, which he lifted from its nest and placed reverently on a nearby metal table. He withdrew to what he considered to be a discreet distance and waited for the detectives to complete their work.

It was encased in several folds of plain cotton, and even before Jarrett unwrapped it he knew it was something of great worth. For one thing, it was small, yet heavy, which suggested only one possible material. As he laid back the last layer he found that he had uncovered a gleaming gold lion, erect on its hind legs and clawing at the air. The pin and keeper on the rear of the object were old in style but still firm and engaged positively.

'One of the Western Bank box holders mentioned a specific item,' he said, then waited while Charlie Grant looked through the notes he had taken from Russell's report.

'Cyrus Brand, Parkfield House, Superintendent,' the inspector replied. 'A gold brooch in the form of a lion. May be plated.'

'Well, this looks like gold, all right, and it is in the form of a lion. It is too much of a coincidence.'

'The tattoo on the arm of the corpse, you mean?'

'Exactly. The Royal Engineers. Although what an army regiment would do with a gold trinket like this is anybody's guess.' Jarrett carefully rebound the object and placed it in his coat pocket. Then he addressed the assistant manager. 'Tell me, Mr Halliwell, what is the correct procedure if a customer should lose his safe deposit box key?'

'Well, we do have a duplicate, of course. Sometimes holders lose their keys, but more often they fail to pay the rental and the contents fall to the bank.'

'And can you find out how much time is left on this particular box?'

'I will have to check that with the manager, sir. If you give me a moment.'

When the assistant manager returned with the information that the box rent had just been paid, Henry Jarrett was in the process of locking the container. He then tucked the key away once more in his fob pocket.

'You may return it to its correct location, Mr Halliwell,' the superintendent said, adding, 'should anyone claim to have mislaid the key to this box I want you to notify me at once. Not the following day or whenever it suits your Mr Botfield, but at once. Do I make myself clear?'

'Absolutely, sir.'

'Good.' Jarrett beamed at him for being so helpful. 'I am very much obliged.'

★ ★ ★

'To be perfectly honest,' Lizzie said, when she and Jeannie were ferrying the peelings and ash buckets to the midden, 'I didn't for a moment imagine you being interested in bettering yourself.'

'Well there's cheek if I ever heard it.' Jeannie gave her a dirty look. 'I went to the church school.'

'So did I, but there's church schools and church schools.'

'Yes, but mine was a good one.'

'Oh, you'd say that anyway.' Lizzie stated, and scurried back inside for another bucket, leaving Jeannie to rake the waste level in the compost heap. Almost immediately, she was back. 'If your school was so good why do you want this improvement nonsense?'

135

'To better my chances of landing a gent.' Jeannie adopted her impassive, take-it-or-leave-it expression. 'No man wants a dunce for a wife.'

'And what man is going to marry a skivvy?'

'I'm not a skivvy. Mrs Maitland was particular about that when she took me on.'

'All right,' Lizzie said, 'not a skivvy, but a maid of all work.'

'Lots of them. Don't you read your *Servant's Magazine?*'

'Yes, but you can't believe it all.'

'I don't agree.' Jeannie considered her disdainfully for a few seconds, before bursting into laughter. 'If you are going to be the mistress of a big house you have to know all about money. And you must keep an eye on the kitchen, the wine cellar and the silver.'

'You have got a big notion for yourself,' Lizzie proclaimed. 'Big house, indeed. Poorhouse, more like.'

'Don't you believe it. As soon as I start the improvement class you'll see a big difference.' Jeannie produced a twice-folded square of newsprint from her pinny pocket and held it out for Lizzie to take. 'I cut that out of the paper when the gentlemen had finished with it. I'm going to go on Friday, my day off.'

Lizzie scanned the advertisement.

'*PROFESSOR EUSEBIUS BECK,*' she said, shaking her head. '*CORINTHIAN HALLS EVERY MONDAY, WEDNESDAY AND FRIDAY.*'

'Carry on,' Jeannie urged.

'THE LATEST SWIFT MEANS OF EDUCATING THE MIND THROUGH MESMERISM. VISIT THE MYSTIC LABORATORY AND EXPERIENCE NATURAL MAGIC. NOW FOR THE FIRST TIME PROFESSOR BECK WILL SUSPEND HIS ASSISTANT, MISS AMELIA MOFFAT, SOME FEET IN THE AIR BY MEANS OF CONDENSED CHLOROFORM! DOORS OPEN AT 7 P.M. COME IN IGNORANCE AND DEPART IMPROVED.'

'Well?' Jeannie demanded. 'Are you converted?'

'I certainly am not.' Lizzie returned the clipping to its owner. 'Would you let a complete stranger mesmerize you?'

'And why not, if it improves the mind? You're just too smart for your own good, Lizzie Gill, and I don't mean a smart brain.'

'Oh, is that so? Well, if you had any sense you would ask Mrs Maitland what she thinks of that before going and doing something silly.'

'She is bound to tell me not to do it, because it isn't in her interests for us to seek betterment. It suits her just fine to keep us as we are.'

'Superintendent Jarrett, then,' Lizzie suggested. 'He'll tell you what he thinks in no uncertain terms.'

'No, I am going to see to this myself. I almost wish I hadn't told you now.'

'Oh, don't worry, I won't tell anyone if you don't want me to.'

'Promise?'

'Of course I promise. If you want to do something daft that's your affair.'

★ ★ ★

For all their wealth, the early West Indian and Carolinian plantation owners and merchants continued to live in the same old tenements they had been born into. Every day after adding to their fortunes they would climb those creaky stairs and dine on plain fare. But their sons saw things differently and built the mansion houses like Parkfield, set amid fifteen tree-studded acres on the south side of the river.

Henry Jarrett climbed down from the wagonette, gave PC Jamieson a nod which was supposed to convey how long he was going to be, and ascended the gleaming white steps to a door that seemed to open by magic.

Unlike most town houses, Parkfield employed a veritable army of servants, from skivvies and stable boys to the butler, housekeeper and footmen who bolstered up this privileged world. Yet few were in evidence as the tall, dark-skinned retainer led the superintendent through the echoing, marble-floored hall to a large lounge.

Cyrus Brand, fourth generation of a family whose fortune had been based on Jamaican sugar, stood before an Adam fireplace that was fully his own height. His expression suggested that he did not know whether to be pleased or concerned at this unexpected visit from the police.

'Superintendent Jarrett,' he declared, then returned the not inexpensive *carte de visite* so that it might be used again for further introductions. 'Please make yourself comfortable.'

After establishing that the kitchen did not actually have Black Dragon tea, and furthermore had never heard of it, Jarrett happily accepted a cup of excellent Jamaican coffee.

'You must be wondering why I have called upon you, Mr Brand,' he said warmly.

'Well, Parkfield is quite a distance from the city centre,' Brand observed, taking a seat on the other side of a highly polished table. 'Strictly speaking, does this area not fall under the jurisdiction of the Gorbals police?'

'We took them over.' The superintendent

beamed broadly. 'It was called a merger to avoid hurting anyone's feelings.'

'I see, but that still doesn't explain why a superintendent of detectives would cross the river, when I am sure you have no end of problems to deal with.'

'Indeed I have, and the Western Bank robbery is not the least of them.' Jarrett could tell that Cyrus Brand was waiting for the matter to be raised and didn't blink an eyelid when it was finally mentioned. 'According to Detective Constable Russell, who was on duty during the initial period just after the discovery of the break-in, your actions were, shall we say, memorable.'

'I was dreadfully upset, Superintendent,' Brand answered frankly. 'I don't often lose control of my emotions, but on that occasion I had great cause to do so.'

'I can't see why. I understand that several items were overlooked by the thieves, and that you told Russell that such objects as were taken were of no great worth.'

'Absolutely correct.' Brand paused briefly, then said, 'I am a budding collector, sir, and as such attach great importance to my pieces. You could compare it to the wild fanaticism of the religious convert, who is always and ever a greater thunderer than the man born to the belief.'

'Is that why you were so angry about the off-hand treatment your wooden items had received?'

'I am afraid so. Although they have no intrinsic value, they were the first objects I acquired and the very core of my collection.'

'Which is?'

'Church artefacts.' Brand smiled thinly. 'I could bore you to death with the story of how I came to be an enthusiast, but I fear it would serve no useful purpose.'

'I am not altogether sure that is true, Mr Brand,' the superintendent said, though not sincerely. 'Just tell me why you were so concerned that someone may have touched what Russell described as wooden tiles.'

'Altar decorations, actually,' Brand corrected. 'I suppose it was the thought of my precious collection being thrown onto the rubble that caused me to explode, Superintendent.'

'I can quite understand that, but why did you demand to know if they had been handled?'

'That was very unreasonable of me, I know.' Brand looked thoroughly abashed. 'Ancient items should be touched as little as possible if they are to last, but these appeared to have been treated in a most cavalier way. As I said, I merely lost control.'

Jarrett decided to switch tack then.

'You also mentioned a gold brooch,' he said.

'Yes, the lion.' Brand shrugged lightly. 'Have you found it?'

'As a matter of fact we have,' Jarrett produced the wrapped item and carefully uncovered it. 'Is this the object in question, Mr Brand?'

'Absolutely!' A delighted Cyrus Brand accepted the brooch and polished it lightly with his handkerchief. 'It would only fetch ten or twenty pounds at best, but it means so much to me. Does this mean that you have caught the thief?'

'I am sorry, Mr Brand, but I am not at liberty to divulge that information.'

'No, of course not. Very foolish of me.' Brand waited while the retainer entered, poured the coffees with all due ceremony, then departed and closed the double doors behind him. 'Forgive me, Superintendent Jarrett, but I haven't been quite as candid as you might think.'

'I had a feeling you might be keeping something back,' Jarrett admitted.

'As indeed I was. If you will excuse me for a moment, Superintendent, I will be right back.'

'Yes, of course.'

Brand rose quickly and left the room, leaving Jarrett to try to guess what was coming next. But before he could even begin to marshal his thoughts, the tall man was back and this time he was carrying a leather wallet secured by a blue ribbon. He took his seat once more, drew open the bow and somewhat reverently lifted the flap.

'Bearer bonds,' he said.

Henry Jarrett accepted the documents he was being offered.

'You will have to explain the principle to me,' the superintendent admitted.

'It is really quite straightforward. These bonds are purchased by investors who, for one reason or another, do not wish their identities to be known to anyone.' Brand paused briefly, then added, 'The only drawback to bearer bonds, sir, is that they are not registered. There is no record of ownership or transactions, which means that whosoever holds those bonds in his hands owns them.'

Jarrett laughed. 'Which briefly makes me very wealthy indeed, Mr Brand,' he said. 'You are very trusting, sir.'

'Know your man, Superintendent, that's what I say. And I know you for a straight fellow.'

Henry Jarrett was as prone to flattery as the

next man, but his years in Hong Kong, where it was expected, had taught him to keep his feet firmly on the ground and to immediately change the subject.

'So you have invested fifty thousand pounds in a transatlantic shipping company at the height of the American war,' he observed. 'Was that quite wise, Mr Brand?'

This time it was Cyrus Brand's turn to be amused.

'The tide has turned, no pun intended,' he said warmly. 'The Union will be victorious and this city will be among the first to take advantage of that.'

'Well, thank you for letting me see the bonds,' Jarrett said, returning the documents to Brand who put them carefully away in the folder. 'However, I still don't quite see what they have to do with your concern over the Western Bank incident.'

'Oh, I think you will, when I tell you that these bonds were in my safe deposit box until two days before the robbery. My outburst was more one of relief than anger, sir. Had a sudden impulse not required me to remove them I would have lost everything.'

'That I can well understand,' Jarrett said. 'Do you think the thieves were after the bonds?'

'I can't see how they could have known

about them, yet it almost looks that way.'

'How many people know about your speculative investment?'

'Nobody but myself and the London dealer I purchased them from.'

'Household staff?'

'Good Heavens, no. I never discuss anything with the domestics.' Brand shook his head vigorously, as though denying even the faintest possibility of their understanding such things let alone profiting from them. 'The documents had rested in the safe deposit box right up until I brought them home.'

'I know it is rather a foolish observation to make, particularly in view of what happened, but did you not feel that they were much safer where they were?'

'I really don't know why I withdrew the bonds, Superintendent, but I did and that is all there is to it. Perhaps it was a premonition.'

'They do say such things happen.' Jarrett finished his coffee and rose to his feet in preparation for taking his leave. His work here was finished. 'Good luck with your investment, Mr Brand, and with your collection.'

PC Jamieson knocked out the last bright embers from his clay jaw-warmer and, having made sure that no glow remained, tucked it safely away. It wouldn't have been the first time he had set fire to his coat pocket.

*   *   *

Rather than making directly for Mrs Maitland's superior guest house for respectable single gentlemen, Henry Jarrett called in at Gowrie's Nursery behind the saw pit in Bell Square that evening to purchase a new item for his Wardian case. He had been reading about the Rock Brake, or Parsley Fern, and fancied including a small example on his miniature mountain. Thus it was that he once more found himself upstairs on the Menzies horse-bus with a small potted fern carefully perched on his knee. A gentleman does not carry flowers in public, or even in private, but foliage alone is a recognized exception, so Jarrett attracted no funny looks at all on his journey home.

Not that he was unduly mindful of what his fellow passengers were thinking. He had quite enough to dwell on without considering such trivia. Problems were piling up and solutions were not forthcoming, so perhaps a few minutes planting and contemplation would achieve what trying to force answers could not.

The round of beef went down a treat and was even more plentiful than usual, owing to Albert Sweetman's continued absence. So by the time Jarrett reached his blessed retreat he was inclined to stretch out on the bed for a short time before planting his new acquisition. But if the body rested the mind did not.

The blunt and unpalatable truth was that he had two murders on his hands and not even the faintest notion of who had carried them out. That they were positively connected had been demonstrated by the nature of the weapon used, while the fact that both men once belonged to the same regiment suggested a further link. Hadden had been an officer in the Royal Engineers and the latest victim appeared to have been a sapper, more than familiar with trench and tunnel building, but did that prove they had both been present at the Western Bank robbery, or did he, Jarrett, merely wish it to be so because he had nothing else?

And what about the others? He had reasoned that the optimum number of actual workers was three, with a supervisor or lookout controlling their efforts. Theoretically, two diggers could have done it, but the clearing away and stacking of spoil would have been more efficiently carried out, as he and Charlie Grant had agreed, by having one at the working face, another removing the waste and a third stacking, and no doubt rotating these tasks at regular intervals. If that was so, then there were two men out there who were either, or both, responsible for the murder of their cohorts, or were at risk from another party who may have masterminded the entire operation and was now severing all links.

When no answer seemed possible without further information, his thoughts drifted to Mrs Bisley and the probable danger to her very existence, of which she was no doubt entirely unaware. Yet without proof positive of her son's murderous ambitions, she would never listen to one word being said against him. She was his mother, after all, and was no doubt blissfully unaware of the fact that her love was probably not fully reciprocated. But the longer she stood between him and what he no doubt saw as his rightful inheritance, the greater the danger.

Despite Dr Hamilton's warning that Alexander Bisley had friends in high places, friends who would protect him and block any enquiry into the death of his uncle, Jacob French, the life of Seraphina Bisley had to be safeguarded. But what would it take to persuade Chief Constable Rattray to agree with him that French's body ought to be exhumed? For only then could the order be obtained.

It was when he was planting the Rock Brake in a cleft on the chosen and most appropriate background mountain that it occurred to him.

8

It was Jarrett's reasoning that a visit by a senior police officer to the Bisley home might scare Alexander into doing something that could inhibit the investigation. If the man was at all normal he had to be in a state of heightened awareness, if not anxiety, so it was perfectly feasible that he might have more than just considered the possibility of an exhumation. He was a sensible man who must know that the police check the poisons books in the city's chemist shops, and had been even more vigilant since Madeleine Smith. The last thing Jarrett needed was for this man to pull whatever strings were necessary to prevent an order being signed.

That was why Tommy Quinn made two entirely spurious visits to villas on Alder Avenue before arriving at the large front door of Rosebank House and presenting his brass badge to a girl in one of those nice new uniforms, now all the rage from Land's End to John O'Groats and which had been introduced to put young women like her firmly in their place and prevent them from emulating their betters. The odious practice of copying the mistress's garments in cheap material and emulating her mannerisms had gone just far enough and had to be firmly curtailed.

'Sergeant Quinn, Detective Department,' he said, smiling. 'I'm investigating a burglary in the neighbourhood and would like a few words with your master.'

'He's not at home, sir. He's never at home through the day.'

'Your mistress, then.'

'I'll ask, sir, if you'll just wait right there. I don't know what the rule is with coppers.'

Quinn grinned broadly.

'Where are you from?' he asked.

'Wicklow.' She glanced over her shoulder to make sure that no one saw her being familiar with anybody or anything. 'I know where you're from.'

'Now, you're not supposed to volunteer more than you're asked for.'

'Oh, bugger that,' she whispered. 'You're not a toff.'

She disappeared for a full two minutes, then was back to escort him into a drawing room that dwarfed the young lady who sat alone on a large, floral-patterned settee, her embroidery ring now resting on her lap. At first glance Tommy thought she was a child, but it quickly became apparent that she was merely petite, a physical condition accentuated by her light blonde hair and porcelainlike skin.

'Please take a seat, Sergeant Quinn,' she said softly. 'My aunt is resting at the moment and cannot see you, I'm afraid.'

'That's perfectly all right, Miss — ?'

'Healey,' she said. 'Jennifer Healey. I am Mrs Bisley's companion.'

'The lady is unwell?'

'She is no longer young, sir, and Mr French's death has affected her very badly. Ever since her husband passed away, she has relied on Mr French's kindness and generosity.' Miss Healey stopped then and looked somewhat abashed. 'Excuse me, Sergeant. I talk too much sometimes. My cousin Alexander tells me it is a risky habit and one I must guard against.'

It occurred to Tommy that he was also in danger of knowing more than he ought.

'Is he the master of the house?' he asked.

'Yes. My late mother was sister to Mr French and Mrs Bisley. She and my father died at sea some years ago. It is one of those situations where there are few offspring, since Alexander and I are only children and Jacob French never married.'

That, Tommy Quinn thought, was as much as Superintendent Jarrett would need to convince himself once and for all that he was right. This household reeked of wealth and with the complete absence of an extended family, it was the perfect environment for murder.

The trick now would be to keep Miss Healey talking without appearing to be interrogating her.

'What you tell me is extremely interesting,' he said. 'I am investigating a burglary in the area, so it is important that I should know the sort of property that might be vulnerable. Do you have many servants?'

'No, there is only Netta the maid, Mrs Robbins the cook, and Harold, who is Mr Bisley's personal manservant and driver. Town houses do not usually carry as many of a staff as country halls.'

Tommy Quinn gave this some thought, and was tempted to enquire about Mrs Bisley and the nature of her illness, but friendly and informative though Miss Healey was, even she must question his interest in matters that had no bearing on his immediate task. How the old lady's welfare could in any way be related to the fictitious spate of burglaries in the district was quite beyond him. But that wouldn't prevent Superintendent Jarrett from expecting more than he was able to deliver.

'Well, I thank you for your kind cooperation, Miss Healey,' he said, as he prepared to take his leave. 'And please don't concern yourself about the thieves. We will have them before much longer.'

As expected, the maid was waiting in the hallway to attend his departure, but Tommy could see that there was much more on her mind than that. As he closed the large double doors behind him she beckoned him near.

'It's all right,' she said softly. 'there's no one else here at the moment.'

'Have you something to tell me?'

'No, I've got something to ask you.' She paused briefly, then added, 'You look a decent sort. Would you like to take me to the theatre tonight?'

For a few moments Sergeant Quinn's thoughts reeled as he tried to come to terms with this, the last thing he expected.

'You?' he began. 'What I mean is — '

'Oh, don't bother with formalities. I know you're going to tell me it isn't my place, and all that nonsense, but the truth is that Harold the driver was to take me to the Whitebait Theatre tonight, but now Mr Bisley has decided to go to his club and wants him at the ribbons.'

'Another night, then.'

'That's the thing. It's Irish comic songs and

I only have this one evening. And as you know they won't let an unaccompanied female in.'

With his landlady Mrs Grogan's stern face looming up in his thoughts, Tommy Quinn's first inclination was to refuse, mainly because he was firmly of the belief that it was not the girl's place to lead. Yet here was a golden opportunity to find out much more about the household than he ever could otherwise.

'To tell the truth,' he said, 'I can't be sure that I have the evening off. The superintendent could throw anything in my direction.'

'I can understand that,' the girl said, 'so I'll tell you what I'll do. If you don't meet me at the horse-bus stance at the Crescent by seven o'clock, I'll just come back here and huff.'

'Which I'm sure you do very well. But let's hope it doesn't come to that.' He waited until she had drawn open the door to the street, then said, 'I believe you are known as Netta.'

Somehow, that seemed to please her.

'Miss Healey told you that, did she? Well, do I have to call you Sergeant?'

'Tommy Quinn,' he said.

'Netta Byrne.'

★ ★ ★

Superintendent Jarrett and Inspector Grant were in the head office when Sergeant Quinn returned from Rosebank House and told them about his arrangement with the maid. Strictly speaking, it was going to be in his own time and not open to discussion, but a tacit understanding existed in the Detective Department that whatever needed to be done was done. Food, entertainment and sleep fitted into whatever was left.

When it was clear that Charlie Grant couldn't stem his natural desire to grin at, and comment upon, this unexpected development, Henry Jarrett pointedly ignored the coarse remarks and said, 'It has potential, Sergeant. Servants can be of enormous use to the law and the criminal fraternity alike, so make the most of it.'

'That's more or less what I was trying to convey,' Charlie Grant said, still smirking, 'but nobody is listening to me.'

'You may wonder why, Inspector.'

'The question is, Superintendent,' Tommy Quinn ventured, 'how much can she be told?'

'Ideally, nothing, but as soon as you begin to delve she is going to know that we are interested in Bisley. Don't underrate the maids' grapevine. She almost certainly knows that there has been no spate of burglaries in the area, and she is going to want to find out

156

what you are really up to.'

'You don't think she is working for Bisley, sir?'

'She is already working for Bisley, Sergeant, but I understand what you mean. No, these girls accumulate information for their own use. It is a form of currency, useful for trading with others of their ilk.'

'So you wouldn't recommend any reference to arsenic or any other method of removing unnecessary relatives?'

'No, certainly not.' Jarrett considered this briefly. 'If you have to say anything, make it financial irregularities. It's a suitably vague term that covers a multitude of sins.'

★ ★ ★

Irish comic songs were never to Tommy Quinn's liking, but he had to admit that Miss Bradley and Mr O'Grady gave rollicking, full-blooded performances, even on occasions drowning out the very audience itself. But all good things must come to an end, and soon Netta Byrne and he were mingling with the rest of the entertainment seekers in the dark and dangerous canyon that was St Enoch's Wynd. But there was safety in numbers and very soon they had reached Howard Street and the horse-bus stance.

Until that point Tommy had not tried to extract any information about the Bisley household from the girl, but now that they were on board the omnibus and in under twenty minutes or so he would have missed his opportunity, he said slyly, 'I'll bet you hear everything that goes on in Rosebank House.'

Netta giggled.

'Wouldn't you like to know?'

'Why not? We all like a bit of scandal.'

'Oh, I don't know about scandal as such, but it's certainly a strange place. Not at all homely, if you know what I mean.'

'Toffs' houses rarely are.'

'Yes, but Rosebank can be quite scary sometimes. It's nothing you could put a finger on, but Mr Bisley has an icy way about him.'

'Are you thinking of anything in particular?' Tommy asked.

'Well, he has a strange taste in ornaments for one thing. He has an African mask and crossed spears on the wall of his study. Harold the driver says he bought it in a saleroom in West Nile Street.' Netta shrugged lightly. 'I suppose men like that sort of thing.'

'I don't,' Tommy admitted. 'Anyway, my landlady wouldn't allow it.'

'I'm glad to hear it.' Netta was thoughtful for a few moments, then added, 'Also, when I say he is icy, he speaks about his concern for his mother's health, while at the same time he is calm and distant. If I was in his position I would be worried and probably show it.'

'The gentry are taught to hide their feelings.'

'I know that, but even Harold says he's a cool customer. Never talks, he says. It's as though he's always thinking about something and won't let anything or anyone interrupt. Even when they're sitting at the table Miss Healey and he never speak. I wouldn't like that.'

Concerned that he might be taken as being too inquisitive, Tommy paused for a few moments and made a show of checking his pocket watch, but the utterly impassive conductor pointedly ignored this and continued to wait for the exact moment to signal the driver.

'Is Mrs Bisley suffering from any particular illness?' Tommy enquired at length.

'Not as far as I know. I heard Dr Foley telling Mr Bisley that she is weak and needs rest, and that beef tea is as good a remedy as any potion.'

'Who prepares it for her?'

As soon as he said this a twinkle came into Netta's eyes that told him he wasn't fooling anyone.

'Why do you want to know, Tommy?' She asked. 'You think Mr Bisley's up to no good, don't you?'

'I was just being curious. Nosey if you like.'

'No, it's more than that. I knew when you were talking to Miss Healey that it had nothing to do with burglaries. If there had been anything like that in the district I would have heard about it. Us maids have our own telegraph, you know.'

'Yes, I'm sure you have.' Tommy raised an eyebrow in his most theatrical manner. 'So you were listening at the door, were you?'

'That's what they're made for, isn't it?' Netta fell silent, but only briefly. 'Well? Are you going to tell me what it's all about?'

'First, you tell me who makes the beef tea.'

'Mrs Robbins does, and either Miss Healey or myself feeds her. We usually take turn about, so that Mrs Bisley can have a fresh face to look at.'

'Does Mr Bisley ever administer to his mother?'

'He always goes up to see her when he comes home at night, but he never gives her the beef tea. That wouldn't be a gentleman's job, anyway.'

'What does he think of Miss Healey?'

'Not much, I would say. She is also a servant, remember. You should know that,

160

Tommy. Governesses and companions are between stairs and mix with neither.'

'But she's family.'

'Not in Mr Bisley's opinion. A poor cousin doesn't rank very highly.'

'That's very sad.'

'Oh, don't worry about her. Miss Healey is a pleasant soul, but perfectly capable of looking after herself.' Netta shrugged lightly. 'She'll have to, if anything happens to Mrs Bisley, because I heard him telling Miss Healey that her continued existence in the house depended on his mother's welfare.'

★　★　★

Tommy Quinn's report to Superintendent Jarrett was short and to the point. Unless he had seriously misread the situation, Alexander Bisley was a cold-blooded individual who had either already embarked on a second murder, or was about to. Jennifer Healey may believe that her aunt had been weakened by the strain of losing her brother, and Dr Foley no doubt placed great faith in his beef tea, but the blunt truth was that Bisley was almost certainly administering arsenic to his mother in gradual amounts, just as he probably did in the case of his late uncle. He had purchased a quite sufficient amount, after all.

Since medical protocol forbade the questioning of Foley's diagnosis or competence, there was only one course left open to Henry Jarrett if Seraphina Bisley was not to follow Jacob French into the land of the Great Majority.

★　★　★

Chief Constable Rattray rose slowly from his seat and, still reading the unbelievable words on the paper Jarrett had given him, crossed to the window where the brightness of the day might somehow illuminate both the page and his confused thoughts.

'Have you gone quite mad?' he demanded, glaring at the superintendent. 'Alexander Bisley is a very senior figure in several institutions. You are asking me to seek authorization for the exhumation of his uncle on the strength of absolutely nothing.'

'Not nothing, sir,' Jarrett protested. 'As you can see, Bisley purchased a three-shilling packet of arsenic a suspiciously short time before the death of his uncle.'

'And made no attempt to hide the fact.'

'Indeed, but if he had used an alias and been found out it would have gone very badly for him.'

Rattray threw the note onto the large desk

and rested heavily on his knuckles.

'You have no evidence of wrongdoing whatsoever, Jarrett,' he growled. 'The answer is no.'

'I sincerely wish you would reconsider, sir,' the superintendent objected. 'We really do require this.'

The CC frowned deeply as he tried, and failed, to understand what Jarrett had just said.

'How in the name of hell can we possibly require such a thing?' he demanded.

'To deflect the press, sir.'

'Explain.'

'Certainly, sir. We have two murders on our hands, and very little to go on. If I am right, that is not the last of it. I have every reason to believe that other members of the gang may fall foul of what appears to be a rival group.'

'But that would be bloody catastrophic.'

'Yes, it would, sir,' Jarrett said, then quickly added, 'unless the papers had a bigger and better bone to chew on.'

'An unfortunate choice of words, superintendent, but I see what you are thinking.'

'Excellent, sir. If we exhume Jacob French and demonstrate that he was poisoned, we can arrest Bisley and make the announcement immediately. At that moment, sir, not one of those wolves will be even remotely interested in the criminals who carried out the robbery. Even the Western Bank will be forgotten.'

'Except by you, I hope.'

'Of course, sir. My men and I will be able to turn all of our attention to retrieving the stolen property, and by the time the Bisley affair has begun to lose its interest they will find it difficult to pick up the trail, so to speak.'

'Not bad, Jarrett,' the CC said, sparing him a rare smile, 'not bad at all. I think perhaps we should get in touch with Sheriff Allison at once.'

'I believe the family can object, sir.'

'Only if they know about it. Are you going to tell them?'

'No, sir.'

'Good man, Jarrett. That's what I like.'

★　★　★

Tommy Quinn had just returned from a wasted trip to the records room, where absolutely nothing incriminating about Alexander Bisley was to be found, when Henry Jarrett came down from the gods.

'Any luck, sir?' the sergeant enquired.

'Unless the sheriff objects, we have our

exhumation order for Jacob French's remains.'

Suddenly, there was a sharp rap at the door and the uninvited, fresh face of a new recruit appeared as if out of a lamp.

'A message from Inspector Grant for you, sir,' the boy said happily. 'He is in the interview room with a woman who has mislaid a husband.'

'Hers?'

'Presumably, sir. Do you want me to ask him?'

'It was a joke, boy. Perhaps I shouldn't make them if they are not going to be appreciated.'

Followed rapidly by Sergeant Quinn, who was still mulling over the previous night, and at the same time temporarily at a loss to know what to do next in the Megan Speirs matter, Henry Jarrett made his way to the interrogation room and found Charlie Grant still in his coat and with his hat on the table.

'This young woman was waiting in the front hall when I arrived, Superintendent,' he said. 'Ellie Goudie's the name. Husband Neil Goudie has been absent for a couple of nights now.'

Jarrett took one of the vacant chairs and positioned it at the end of the table. Mrs Goudie was not a suspect in anything, so having her face a wall of interrogators was neither necessary nor decent.

'Tell me, Mrs Goudie,' the superintendent began, 'is it not possible that your husband merely overdid the refreshments and lost all sense of time?'

'Neil doesn't drink,' she said firmly. That was the first thing Jarrett noticed about her. She was made of solid oak, and although Grant had referred to her as young, the care lines on her face had added a decade to her. That experience and rigidity was going to be well tested shortly. 'He doesn't drink and he doesn't smoke, which is just as well because we haven't got an income.'

'How do you live?'

To Jarrett's relief she said, 'I take in washing. It isn't easy with two wee ones hanging on to you, but it's better than watching them starve to death.'

'Where are the children now?'

'With the woman next door. Mrs Park'll look after them for an hour or two.'

'When did your husband work last?'

'He hasn't had a real job since he left the army. South Africa, India and God knows where else, but it all counted for nothing in the end. There's no greater rubbish than an old soldier.'

Jarrett turned to Quinn then and said, 'Bring the collodion print of man number two.'

Mrs Goudie looked at each of the officers in turn and it was clear that she was far from dim-witted. In fact, she was already preparing herself for the worst.

'He's dead, isn't he?' she said coldly. 'Come on, you can tell me. I've faced that before.'

'Perhaps we should wait before speculating, Mrs Goudie,' Jarrett advised.

'But you have a body, haven't you? Was he in the river?'

'First, we do have a body, but he was not fished out of the river.' The superintendent decided to pursue that line just to see where it led to. 'Why did you think he might have been in the river, Mrs Goudie? Sober men rarely fall into the hands of the Preservation people. Unless, of course — '

'They jump to their deaths.' Ellie Goudie nodded grimly. 'That's what I was meaning. He is a healthy man and no one is going to do him to death for the dust in his pockets. I took it that he decided to depart the world in his own time.'

'I can assure you he was not the instigator of his own death, Mrs Goudie. If indeed it is your husband.'

Then Tommy Quinn was back with a folder and a fresh print taken only the previous evening from the glass collodion negative. Jarrett accepted the print, checked it to make sure it was as tasteful as a corpse with its throat cut could possibly be, then placed it in front of Mrs Goudie. She sat still for quite some considerable time, then asked, 'How did he die?'

'First, Mrs Goudie, is this your husband?'

'Yes, that's Neil, all right.' She pushed the picture away and once more sat bolt upright. There was still not a trace of emotion. Either it had died of poverty or she was unwilling to show her feelings to a bunch of complete strangers. 'Well?'

'He was murdered.'

'But why? He had nothing and he didn't get into drunken fights. Why would anyone waste their time murdering him?'

'Perhaps you could tell us. Did your husband say anything to you about being hired for a particular job?'

'Hired as what?'

'A tunneler. He was a sapper, after all.'

'Now who on earth would want a tunnel?' She was clearly confused. 'Who told you this? If Neil was hired to do anything at all I never saw a farthing of it.'

'All right, I will put it this way. Apart from being missing for two nights, did your husband stay away from home on any other night?'

'Yes, last Saturday. He didn't come back

until first light, but he wouldn't say where he had been. All I could get out of him was things should improve soon. I didn't believe a word of it, and it looks now as though I was right.' Ellie Goudie gave a long sigh. 'He wasn't much use, and at least now I don't have to feed him, so there will be more for the children.'

It occurred to Jarrett that he might prefer a better epitaph than that.

'I am afraid we are going to have to have a positive identification at the City Mortuary,' he said. 'Do you want to get it over with, Mrs Goudie?'

'Why not? But I don't know how I'm going to bury him.'

'The city will take care of that.' Jarrett was anxious to get this over with and saw no good reason for delaying the next stage. It wasn't as though Mrs Goudie was particularly heartbroken or required time to compose herself. 'After the formal identification I'm afraid we are going to have to search your house.'

She stared at him.

'Search?' she repeated. 'For what?'

'That remains to be seen, Mrs Goudie,' Charlie Grant put in. 'We believe that your husband was involved in a robbery on the night you say he didn't come home, so it will

169

be necessary for us to thoroughly examine the property.'

'The property?' she snorted derisively. 'It's a room and kitchen, if you could even call it that. There's nowhere to hide anything.'

'Nevertheless, we have to conduct a search. I'm sorry if it is inconvenient, especially at this time, but it has to be done.'

★　★　★

The blood wagon was there and waiting when the wagonette delivered the four of them to the Black Gates of the City of the Dead — the Necropolis. Their arrival was unannounced, but that was as it should be if they were to avoid the sort of legal entanglements that could cost the life of Seraphina Bisley and deprive a murderer of his just deserts.

First down was Superintendent Henry Jarrett, followed by Sergeant Quinn because Charlie Grant was otherwise employed turning over the Goudie dwelling. Then came Dr Hamilton, whose presence in a supervisory capacity was essential. Lastly, Chief Constable Rattray, never a lover of cemeteries at the very best of times, reluctantly stepped from the four-seater onto the cold, hard cobblestones as though from the tumbrel to the blade.

'You had better be bloody well right, Jarrett,' he grumbled. 'I have staked a hell of a lot on this.'

'And stand to accrue great honours, sir,' Jarrett said.

Rattray looked quizzically at him.

'Was that sarcasm?' he demanded.

'No, sir, I was merely pointing out that as far as the newspapers are concerned, the credit for trapping a killer and saving the life of an innocent woman will be yours alone. It is overdue, don't you think, sir?'

'Yes, well, I have to agree with you on that score.' And with that the CC joined the parade into the cemetery, though with no great enthusiasm and no inclination whatsoever to lead the way. 'Bloody newspapers.'

It was a superintendent of a different shade who met them at the door of the large cottage beyond the gates. James Mitchell had been responsible for the Necropolis for almost twenty years and in that time had seen many arrive and very few leave.

'And what can I do for you, gentlemen?' he partly asked, partly demanded.

CC Rattray held out the printed form.

'Order for exhumation,' he stated flatly, clearly expecting Mitchell to jump to attention. 'Jacob French. His plot number, please.'

But Mitchell was less than impressed.

'Can't help you, I'm afraid. Sorry.'

'What do you mean, sorry? This is an order signed by Sheriff Allison. The plot number, please.'

'Again, I can't help you.' Mitchell's eyes skimmed over the faces of the four men whose next move rested on his compliance. 'I'm not trying to be difficult, gentlemen, but the blunt truth is that Jacob French doesn't have a plot. He wasn't buried.'

For several long seconds confusion reigned, then Henry Jarrett said, 'He is in a tomb, isn't he?'

'Indeed he is, sir. It is in the Greek Ionic style. Small, but tasteful. He had it built at the time of the typhoid outbreak, when it looked as though we were all going to be losers.'

Rattray turned to Dr Hamilton then.

'Where does this leave us, sir?' he asked.

'In a more favourable position, I would say, Chief Constable. For one thing, we won't require the services of Mr Mitchell's gravediggers, so we can attend to matters and depart much more rapidly.'

'But you are sure there is nothing about a tomb that runs counter to an exhumation order?'

'Nothing at all, Mr Rattray.'

'Good.' The CC redirected his attention to Park Superintendent Mitchell. 'It will be locked, I suppose?'

'Sadly forced upon us by the resurrection men, sir.'

'Who holds the key to this particular tomb?'

'I do.'

'And do you have a coffin barrow nearby?'

'I have indeed and a man to go with it.'

'Then summon him and lead the way, Superintendent Mitchell. The sooner we get this matter over with the happier I will be.'

It was a larger caravan that made its way over the Bridge of Sighs above the stream known as the Molindinar. The original four now walked in the wake of Superintendent Mitchell, while a dour individual, who obviously didn't merit a name, brought up the rear with his coffin-long, two-wheeled barrow, which was totally indistinguishable from the drunk barrows used by the police every night in life.

Had they proceeded by the conventional, more circuitous route, it would have taken them at least twenty minutes to reach the sector in which stood the white marble tomb of Jacob French. Mitchell, however, had his own short-cuts, which were little more than a maze of sheep tracks through the shrubbery

173

on the still unused area of the park. In a little under ten minutes they had reached the small Ionic temple, where Superintendent Mitchell quickly turned the key in a large well-oiled padlock and drew back the bronze door.

The coffin sat alone on a dais to the left of the cella. After just a few days the odour of corruption should have been greater, but the tight-fitting lid and cool interior helped to reduce it considerably. It would be a different matter entirely when Dr Hamilton got it back to the City Mortuary and opened it up.

'Better give the barrow man a hand, Sergeant,' Henry Jarrett said. 'Looks a bit on the heavy side.'

Tommy Quinn waited until the barrow had been pushed into the interior of the tomb, noting with a degree of satisfaction that it's bed corresponded quite nicely to the height of the dais, then assisted the nameless worker to slide the casket sideways onto the trolley.

★ ★ ★

If the number 13 was unlucky, then 13a Havannah Street was probably unluckier than 13b. Certainly, Neil Goudie and the woman who was foolish enough to marry him had never experienced one moment's good fortune in this place. Perhaps never in their lives.

Ellie Goudie waved a careless hand.

'Start where you like,' she said. 'I don't know what you're looking for, but you won't find it.'

The house, if it could be called that, consisted of a single room with a curtained bed alcove beneath which was a low, wheeled bed, or 'hurley', that would be drawn out at night for the children or the old folk. Provision for heating and cooking was provided by a Carron hob grate, suggesting that this may once have been a small part of a larger and finer property. Even Charlie Grant, for whom art was a self-indulgent waste of time, could see that the ornate iron flowers and the name of Carron of Falkirk's chief designer, John Adam, did not belong in a place like this.

If the square on the floor had once been a carpet, there was precious little of the wool left and not a great deal of canvas. PC Corrigan tested the twisted floorboards one by one, but couldn't find one loose enough to be lifted with either his fingertips or a penknife. And PC Kane wasn't having much luck, either. The sparse furniture, which consisted of a rough-hewn table and three more or less unbroken chairs, were hiding

175

nothing. The solitary east chair, worn to the point that the horsehair hung out in tufts, might have concealed any number of treasures, but short of taking it apart there was no way of knowing. After a few minutes prodding with a truncheon, it was declared a dead loss.

'Did your husband have any friends, Mrs Goudie?' Inspector Grant asked eventually. 'Did anyone call?'

'Why would they?' Ellie glared at him. 'I told you he didn't drink, and if you don't do that you don't have any friends.'

'What about army chums?'

'What about them? I never saw anyone from the sappers when he was one of them, so I'm hardly likely to now.'

'Very well, Mrs Goudie, let's try to be more specific. Does the name Christopher Hadden mean anything to you?'

She frowned deeply and was evidently willing to give the matter some thought, whereas before she was dismissing his questions out of hand.

'I can't be sure,' she said, biting her lip. 'Did he kill Neil?'

'No, Hadden is dead. We think that the same person who was responsible for his death may also have killed your husband.'

Ellie sat down then, and rested one arm on

the table. Every day was exhausting, but this one had drained her utterly.

'I'd better go and get the wee ones,' she said. 'Mrs Park has looked after them long enough.'

'Just another couple of minutes, if you don't mind.' Inspector Grant watched Corrigan finishing off his search by checking the few bits of coal in the scuttle, while Kane gave the cold ash under the grate a quick rummage with a bent iron poker. 'Try to remember, Mrs Goudie. Did your husband ever refer to Christopher Hadden as his former captain in the Royal Engineers, or, better still, did anyone like that ever come here?'

'No one ever came here.' Again, she fell silent for a short time. 'But I think Neil may have received a letter from someone important like that.'

'Do you still have it?'

'No, he told me it was from an officer, then scrunched it up and threw it into the fire. I don't know why he would do that. Maybe the man wanted to borrow something, but if so he didn't know our condition very well.'

'Or he might have been instructed to destroy the letter after he had read it,' Charlie Grant suggested. 'Your husband was trained to obey orders, Mrs Goudie, so if an officer gave him a specific command he would carry it out.'

★　★　★

Rattray, Jarrett and Tommy Quinn were perfectly happy to remain in the long, white-tiled corridor of the City Mortuary and leave Dr Hamilton to get on with whatever it was he had to do. If the CC hated the Necropolis, he hated this place even more. But it was infinitely better than looking over Hamilton's shoulder, even for the decent glass of whiskey which outsiders are offered to kill the unpleasant smell. None sat; all paced and two of them considered their futures. Only Sergeant Quinn could claim to be obeying orders.

The Marsh test was not unduly difficult but it was infallible, as it had to be if it lay at one end of a legal process which led to the gallows. Samples of fluid taken from Jacob French's corpse were mixed with sulphuric acid and passed through a U-shaped glass tube, at one end of which was a piece of arsenic-free zinc. Should even the slightest trace of arsenic exist, arsine gas would be created. When this gas was ignited it would decompose into arsenic and hydrogen, and if a clean white ceramic bowl was held to the burning jet any arsenic present would leave a silvery-black deposit on the otherwise pristine surface.

Dr Hamilton's reappearance in the corridor brought about an immediate cessation of all perambulating. He held up the bowl so that they could all see the fruits of his labours.

'I am very sorry, gentlemen,' he said in even tones. 'There is absolutely nothing. There is not one iota of arsenic in the body of Jacob French. The man died of heart failure, just as Dr Foley's certificate states.'

Henry Jarrett glanced at young Tommy Quinn and both waited for the explosion that had to come from the direction of Chief Constable Rattray. Oddly, it never did. Instead, his voice was flat and low, as though this was what he had secretly expected.

'Get him back up to his temple, or whatever the hell it is, Jarrett,' he said. 'If you act quickly there is no reason why Alexander Bisley should know what we have done.'

'There is Mitchell, sir.'

'Yes, but you can take care of him. He seems a reasonably intelligent man, perfectly capable of choosing between remaining in his job and becoming a night shite shifter.' Rattray turned then and made for the frosted glass doors that led to the greater world. At least this time he had his brougham waiting for him and not that glorified dog cart Jarrett had to make do with. 'I am now going to see the sheriff and then I think I will spend the rest of the week at my country house. In the unlikely event of your actually catching anybody for anything, you may send me a telegram.'

'There goes a defeated man,' Dr Hamilton observed. 'You don't think he intends to do something foolish, Superintendent?'

'If you mean what I think you do, there is not the remotest possibility. Self-lovers are rarely self-destroyers.'

'How very true,' Hamilton agreed, then said, 'Well, I will get French lidded and ready to go. Thankfully, I did not need to uncrate him, so it will only take me a few minutes.'

9

He was found by a nanny wheeling her ungrateful charge through Glasgow Green just before nine in the morning. Those who had passed this way before her probably thought he was just another dew-soaked drunk, but she had been a nurse and knew the difference between an oblivious boozer and a corpse. Having exchanged pleasantries in Jail Square with her unconfessed admirer, PC Braid, only a few minutes earlier, she wheeled the carriage around and retraced her steps.

It took Braid a few minutes to reach the spot, decide that this was no ordinary death, and make his way to Central and Desk Sergeant Davie Black. Less than thirty minutes after the nanny made her find Inspector Grant and Sergeant Quinn had made an initial examination of the body, agreed that it was an unlawful killing and sent for Dr Hamilton. Superintendent Jarrett, they concluded, would not be interested in this run-of-the-mill crime. But in assuming that they were wrong.

'It was my fault entirely,' Charlie Grant

said. He and Tommy Quinn had been watching Dr Hamilton perform his preliminary examination when Jarrett arrived at the City Mortuary, none too pleased at the way things were going. 'When I saw the notepad in his jacket pocket I took him for a bookie's runner.'

'I'm just as much to blame,' Sergeant Quinn offered. 'I suggested he might have been killed for his takings. It happens, sir.'

'Of course it happens.' Although Henry Jarrett was far from happy, he was still disinclined to get bogged down with petty squabbling. 'So, can you tell me anything about him?'

'He was a newspaper reporter,' Grant said, relieved that nothing more was going to be said about his little mistake. 'According to the book, Vincent Gittens of the *Advertiser*. He may have been one of those leeches who hang around the main hall at the station.'

Dr Hamilton nodded to Jarrett and used his thick pencil to indicate the scissors that were lying on a nearby tray.

'Murder weapon, Superintendent,' he said. 'As I was saying to Inspector Grant, it is refreshing not to be faced with another throat-cutting.'

'They were still in the corpse?' Jarrett asked.

'Yes, a single strike in the back and that was it.'

'So it is your contention that someone followed him and struck him down in the Green?'

'I didn't say that. This man might have staggered on for quite a distance with them in his back before finally succumbing.'

'Can you say how far?'

'Clearly not, but a good few hundred yards anyway. The important thing is that the scissors were not withdrawn, because otherwise he would have bled to death very quickly. If a weapon is left in the wound it acts as a plug, if you care to put it that way.'

'So we could also say that the assailant is not necessarily blood-soaked?'

'Judging by the limited spread on his shirt and jacket, Superintendent,' Dr Hamilton suggested, 'I would say that he or she would perhaps have a smear of blood on the side of the weapon hand, but there would be none of the mess you get when the killer repeatedly stabs the victim while the heart is still pumping.'

'If you had to guess,' Henry Jarrett said, 'would you say that this was intentional or fortuitous as far as the murderer is concerned?'

'Let me put it this way. If you were setting

out to commit murder I hardly think that a pair of scissors would be your ideal choice of implement. No, this is an impulse killing, and the fact that it was achieved with a single, deadly blow points to its being just that. Fury invariably manifests itself in multiple wounds, a veritable onslaught of stabbing or beating.'

'A woman?'

'I would say so.'

'An act of self-protection, perhaps?'

'Or protecting another party. Otherwise it would have been in the chest, not between the shoulder blades.'

Jarrett lifted the scissors and turned them in his fingers until he was gripping them, dagger-style. The first thing that struck him was the weight. They were the kind a tailor might use, or a dressmaker, but were too bulky and heavy for a lady's sewing box. After a few moments he replaced them on the tray and turned his attention to the contents of the pockets.

'What do we have, Inspector?' he asked.

'Well, Superintendent,' Charlie Grant replied, 'we can sort it into three groups. Notebook and pencil stub, money in interesting quantities, and a cheap pewter-cased pocket watch.'

'How much money?'

'That is the important thing. Plainly, he was not killed for gain. We have here three

184

sovereigns taken from his waistcoat pocket, two pounds in mixed silver found in a leather bag in his jacket pocket, and small change to the value of four shillings and seven pence from his trouser pocket.'

'Quite a considerable sum.' Jarrett looked from Grant to Tommy Quinn, but neither could offer an immediate suggestion. 'Was he bribed by someone who needed desperately to stay out of the papers, or could this be construed in any way as honest gain?'

'Perhaps the notebook will provide an answer, sir,' Tommy Quinn offered.

'Perhaps it will.' Jarrett flipped over the well-thumbed pages to find the most recent entries. 'Now, that is curious.'

'Sir?'

'It looks as though our friend here was lurking in your shadow, Sergeant Quinn. According to these notes, he either overheard your conversation with Megan Speirs, or she relayed it to him.'

Tommy Quinn took the proffered notepad, read and reread the relevant section, then passed it to Inspector Grant.

'I can't explain this, Superintendent,' he said. 'Gittens wasn't present when I spoke to the girl and I can't imagine her telling such things to a cheap scratcher.'

'It is one or the other, Sergeant,' Henry

Jarrett said flatly. 'Whether you like it or not, Gittens was close on your trail. He even found out that Miss Speirs had attended Beck's so-called improvement class. Since that is the final entry in the book we must assume that he had only just learned of it.'

'I still maintain that the girl would never tell him the details of what happened to her.'

'She might if he offered her enough money. What does she earn?'

'I don't know, sir. Ten or fifteen pounds a year, I suppose.'

'So this little collection of coins represents half a year's wages. Perhaps he offered to pay her, then reneged after she had divulged her terrible story. Would that not be cause enough for her to grab the scissors and put an end to him?'

'A few points, Superintendent,' Charlie Grant put in, just as Jarrett knew he would. It was the sort of theory that sounded good for a few seconds, but no longer than that. 'She wouldn't have scissors of that weight to hand. Also, if Gittens had shown her the money why didn't she help herself to it after she had killed him?'

'You said a few points, Inspector. That was two.'

'Yes, indeed. It's more than a mile from Miss Monk's house to the spot where Gittens was found. I don't think he could stagger that far with a pair of scissors in his back, and certainly not in broad daylight. I would think a passer-by might just notice such a thing.'

'He might have been dumped there,' Sergeant Quinn said.

'Not impossible,' Dr Hamilton suggested, 'but a corpse is not easy to carry. An injured man can help a little in his own rescue, but a dead one is a bag of bricks.'

'Miss Monk does keep a phaeton and a driver.' Charlie Grant offered.

'True,' Jarrett agreed, but was not entirely enthusiastic.

Buoyed up by this, Tommy Quinn added, 'Why should the girl be the murderess, sir? Dr Hamilton has said that it looked as though the act was committed in defence of another.'

'Miss Monk?'

'Very possibly.'

'Would a lady like that possess a seamstress's equipment? Is it not the case that she would have her clothes made for her by a professional dressmaker?'

'Which one of us is going to tackle the formidable Miss Monk?' Charlie Grant put in. 'And who wants to watch the *Advertiser's* Jake McGovern squirming and lying as he tries to make out that he knew nothing at all about what Gittens was up to?'

'Don't forget Miss Moffat,' Henry Jarrett suggested. 'If you want a party who would do anything to protect her hero, you could do much worse than that one.'

'But the Corinthian Halls are just as far from the place Gittens was found,' Inspector Grant objected, 'and Beck doesn't have a carriage.'

'Nevertheless, we can't rule that pair out. Gittens may have challenged Beck about the attacks on the girls, and I cannot imagine Miss Moffat permitting that to reach the papers.'

'With all due respect, Superintendent,' Tommy Quinn put in, 'I hardly think they would have overlooked this amount of money.'

'Very true, but every possibility must be investigated. And as soon as possible.'

*　*　*

Henry Jarrett had heard a great deal about Jake McGovern, but until that moment had never laid eyes on the man. All newspaper editors are ruthless, and owner-editors even more so. So the superintendent did not quite expect to be greeted by a courteous and disarmingly pleasant and bewhiskered individual of medium height and neat appearance. What he had anticipated was a gruff and probably boozy mandarin with his feet on the desk and pencil behind each ear. McGovern disappointed on all counts.

'Please, Superintendent Jarrett,' McGovern said, indicating an empty chair. 'Obviously this is about Vincent Gittens. I will, of course, help you all I can, but you will have to bear with me. I am still quite shocked, as you may well understand.'

'Murder is always shocking, Mr McGovern,' Jarrett said, 'but never more so than when it strikes nearby. But then that is true of all things.'

'Indeed it is.' The editor held out a silver humidor containing what were no doubt excellent cheroots, but this was politely declined. 'Are you at liberty to tell me how Gittens met his untimely end?'

'I see no reason why not, since it is only right and proper that he should finally grace the pages in a way he never expected. If you want sensation, Mr McGovern, Vincent Gittens was stabbed in the back with a pair of scissors.'

'Good God!' McGovern sat back in his throne and was clearly having difficulty in taking this in. 'I'll wager even he never thought it would come that way.'

'He expected something of the sort?' Jarrett asked.

'I don't know if it was serious, but he seemed to have a very morbid and somewhat melancholy mien about him. I can't say I actually liked the man, Superintendent, but he was good at his job and I respected him for that.'

'Quite, but did he think that someone was out to kill him?'

'I don't know,' McGovern said thoughtfully, then added, 'Was robbery the motive?'

'It doesn't look that way, although we can't say exactly what he had on his person when he was struck down.'

'So his notebook was still in his pocket?'

'It was indeed.'

'Well, perhaps if you let me have it I'll have a better idea of the sort of leads he was following.'

'I'm sorry, Mr McGovern,' Jarrett replied and noted the flicker of annoyance in the man's eyes. 'The book is evidence. It will be returned to you in due course.'

'Quite so. I fully understand.'

'Did he ever say anything to you about specific threats? Did he make enemies?'

'Of course he made enemies. It is in the nature of the job.'

'How long has he been here?'

'He came to me from the *Paisley Courant* a few months ago.'

'Before that?'

'Down south somewhere. He hailed from Manchester originally. But everyone hails from somewhere else, don't they? I'm from Belfast.'

'Where did he reside?'

'87 Pottery Row, but don't ask me where it is. It probably looks as good as it sounds.'

The superintendent now waited for some enquiry regarding the fate of at least five pounds' worth of sovereigns and mixed silver, plus a bit of pocket scrap. When it didn't come it had to mean either that it had nothing to do with the *Advertiser*, or McGovern didn't want to say why his chief reporter was carrying such a small fortune. 'Three sovereigns, two pounds of mixed silver and four shillings and seven pence in small change. That is what Gittens had on his person. Would you like to explain it to me, Mr McGovern?'

'The editor feigned astonishment and went as far as spreading his arms in surrender.'

'I'm afraid you have me there,' he said. 'A bit of luck, possibly?'

'So you didn't give him the money?'

'No, certainly not.'

'That is really quite awkward,' Jarrett said, 'because the lady in the outer office told me that he had signed out just such an amount. I

191

hope you don't mind. I gave it back to her.'

McGovern stared at him for several seconds, then said expansively, 'Oh, that five pounds! Of course, Superintendent, I remember now. Yes, That was for emergency expenses.'

'To cover?'

'Unforeseen costs. Sometimes it is necessary to purchase information, you understand. Some people are dreadfully mercenary.'

'Yes, I have noticed.' Jarrett waited, but when no further illumination was forthcoming he said, 'Well?'

'Sir?'

'What was it for, Mr McGovern? I mean what exactly was it for?'

'Details.'

'Yes, precise details of the attack on Megan Speirs.'

'Who?'

'Mr McGovern, please do not prevaricate further. The final page in Gittens's notebook contains references to the girl and to a possible suspect. But of course this is not the only story contained therein. Now, it must have occurred to you that some desperate party just may have been trying to stop the publication of a particularly damning story, and if this is true Vincent Gittens was only one of two people who could possibly know what it was and needed to be silenced.'

McGovern's expression turned slowly from the mildly bemused to one of staring horror as the full implication of this really sank in.

★ ★ ★

Miss Emily Monk fixed Tommy Quinn with a challenging stare as if daring him to overstep the mark. On the occasion of his earlier visit to the villa on Millburn Avenue she had permitted Megan to speak with him, but this was different. Matters had taken a much more serious turn. Vincent Gittens, for all his sins, had been sent to the world beyond the veil.

'If that was indeed his name, Sergeant,' she said coldly. 'He didn't introduce himself, other than to say he was from some newspaper or another.'

'Did he say what he wanted?' Tommy Quinn asked.

'No, thank goodness, but his intentions were perfectly plain. If you ask me, young man, he is none the worse of being murdered.'

'Nevertheless, Miss Monk, it is still a crime whatever his character. May I take it that you think he had designs on Miss Speirs?'

'Of course he had. The man was a

reprobate. He even offered her money.'

'For her story, surely?'

She made a face and reinforced it with a dismissive wave of a gloved hand.

'I may be what is generally known as a maiden lady,' she said, 'but I am not entirely unaware of the ways of the world. Fortunately, one does not encounter creatures like Gittens very often.'

Quinn had the distinct feeling that he wasn't getting anywhere and that the straightforward approach was called for.

'Do you have a pair of scissors, Miss Monk?' he enquired.

'Of course.' Interestingly, there wasn't a moment's hesitation or a glimmer of surprise. Rather, she reached out to the left and wheeled her small hobby table around between them. She opened the inlaid lid of her Moroccan leather-clad workbox to let him see the contents. Then she added, 'It is quite old, you know.'

The fitted interior, which was lined in red velvet to compliment the box itself, contained a number of different mother-of-pearl handled items and several thread and lace bobbins. But it was the scissors that concerned Quinn.

'Do you have any other scissors?' he asked.

Miss Monk gently closed her treasured box and wheeled the table back into its proper place beside her wing chair.

'No,' she said firmly. Then added, 'Am I right in assuming that scissors played a part in the demise of this creature?'

'I am afraid I am not at liberty to divulge such information,' Sergeant Quinn said.

'You don't have to. Your questions speak for themselves.'

Tommy Quinn ignored this slight and asked, 'How many of a staff do you employ, Miss Monk?'

'I cannot see the relevance,' she said nippily, 'but if it will speed up your departure from my home, there is Cairns, the proverbial Jack-of-all-trades. He is my handyman gardener and can handle the phaeton, which I use occasionally but not enough to justify keeping a driver. Apart from Megan and Cairns, there is Mrs Atkins, the cook, and a scullery maid, Deans. I did have a skivvy until a few weeks ago, but I invested in some home improvements which meant that I no longer needed her services.'

'Thank you, Miss Monk,' Tommy said. 'You have been most helpful. There is only one other thing.'

'I thought there might be.'

'When Gittens took his leave of you, Miss Monk, where was he going?'

'I have absolutely no idea. The last I saw of

him he was running down the avenue in the direction of the fields.'

'Why was he running?'

'Because I had just told him to get out or Cairns would give him a thorough hiding.'

★ ★ ★

Charlie Grant's appearance at. the Corinthian Halls was not entirely unexpected. The nature of Professor Beck's work was such that the arrival of the law was always a possibility, but that was only because the police were unimaginative and blinkered. Services such as the ones he offered were invariably suspect, but that was how it had been through the ages. Forward thinkers are always reviled.

But half-anticipated though the police may have been, Charlie Grant's brass badge was probably the last thing Amelia Moffat wanted to see at that particular moment. The lady stood four-square in front of him, blocking his progress towards the stage and challenging him to outstare her. Even the bright purple dress she was wearing seemed to add to her power.

'I thought we had concluded our business, Inspector,' she said sharply. 'I was under the impression that I had answered your sergeant's questions satisfactorily. Surely you cannot still harbour doubts about the professor's innocence.'

'That's not exactly why I'm here, Miss Moffat.' Grant looked around but there was no Eusebius Beck to be seen. 'What can you tell me about Vincent Gittens?'

'Never heard of the man.'

'That's strange, because he seems to have heard of you. Or at least of your hero, Beck.'

'Inspector, I don't like your tone, and it goes without saying that I don't like you.'

'I can't say that troubles me unduly, Miss Moffat. What you think of me pales into insignificance compared to my opinion of that charlatan, Beck.'

Far from backing away from the one she must have perceived as something of a threat, Amelia Moffat advanced on Charlie Grant to the point where he could quite easily persuade himself that she had done away with the newspaperman. When she stopped it was well within arm's reach and he found himself wondering how many pairs of scissors she possessed.

'I would be grateful if you would state your business,' she said coldly, 'then get out and leave us alone.'

'It looks to me as though you are alone, Miss Moffat.'

'Not entirely.'

Instinctively, Charlie Grant looked upwards into the pallid, expressionless face of the man on the gantry. The thin fingers were gripping the rail and he was staring directly downward into the inspector's eyes. Yet when he spoke his voice was gentle and soft.

'You must forgive Miss Moffat,' Eusebius Beck said. 'She is wonderfully protective and I really do not know what I should do without her.'

'Was she being protective when she dealt with Vincent Gittens?' Grant asked.

Beck did not reply immediately, but descended slowly and cautiously to the stage.

'That is the second time you have used that name, Inspector Grant,' he said, 'and I can only repeat what Miss Moffat told you. I — we — have never heard of a Vincent Gittens. Who is this person anyway?'

Grant didn't reply, but instead asked, 'Do you have a pair of scissors?'

'I should imagine most people have scissors.' The thin man turned then to his assistant. 'Miss Moffat, would you please fetch them for the inspector.'

When Amelia Moffat had swished off to carry out Beck's bidding, Grant said, 'It's interesting that you didn't ask why, Mr Beck. It is as though you already knew, so I would venture to suggest that Miss Moffat will return with the excuse that she has mislaid the items.'

Not for the first time, Charlie Grant was to be proved wrong. Amelia Moffat was back within a minute with a pair of bright scissors which she held by the blades, while offering him the black-japanned loop handles.

Inspector Grant took them and examined them closely.

'New,' he observed. 'When did you buy them?'

'A few weeks ago,' Miss Moffat said. 'We use them a great deal for our decorations and the ones we had were very blunt.'

'Why not use the services of a grinder?'

'They are never the same as a fresh pair of Sheffield scissors,' Eusebius Beck put in. 'Would you please tell Miss Moffat and me what we are supposed to have done?'

Once more Charlie Grant ignored the question.

'I would like to know where you bought these,' he said. 'If possible, please tell me exactly when it was and how much you paid for them. A receipt would be ideal.'

10

'Shot me with my own bolt,' Charlie Grant announced when he joined Superintendent Jarrett and Sergeant Quinn in the main office. 'I asked Miss Moffat to produce a receipt for a replacement pair of scissors she recently bought, and the damned woman did just that. Murray's Drysalters & Hardware in the Trongate; 1/9d the pair, bought twelve days ago.'

'Unless she could foresee the necessity of stabbing Gittens,' the superintendent said, 'that would seem to let her out. Yet I am not happy with it. She may have used the old ones on him.'

'I thought about that, but it doesn't ring true. I think we agree that it was probably a sudden, desperate act rather than a premeditated killing. If she had scissors to hand they would be the new ones, wouldn't they? You don't purchase new scissors and leave them in a drawer for some time before using them. You buy them because you need them there and then.'

Jarrett then asked, 'Sergeant Quinn, what about Miss Monk?'

'She didn't kill Gittens,' Tommy Quinn said. 'She is the sort who would tell you if she had done. She doesn't seem to be afraid of anything and certainly not the police. No, I am quite satisfied that Gittens left Millburn Avenue on the run, just as Miss Monk said.'

'Did you have a word with her driver, Cairns?'

'Yes, just to confirm the story. I wouldn't call him a bully-boy, but he could certainly dish it out if it came to the bit.'

Jarrett considered it for a few moments then said, 'The greater likelihood is that Gittens was killed either by Eusebius Beck or Miss Moffat.'

'So how do you see it happening, sir?'

'I could be quite wrong, but I would suggest that Gittens possibly accused Beck of something that threatened his liberty or well-being, and that Amelia Moffat grabbed up her nice new shears and rescued her lord and master from the ruination he so richly deserves.'

'Then, sir?'

'Then Beck, being as informed as he is, would undoubtedly tell her what would happen if the scissors were pulled out of the wound. At that point, Gittens may have been alive or dead. If the former, it is not impossible that he staggered off as Dr

Hamilton has suggested, but I really don't subscribe to that. I think between them they manhandled his corpse out of the house, if that is where the crime occurred, and somehow delivered it to Glasgow Green, where they left him unceremoniously in the long grass.'

'Delivered how, Superintendent?'

'Well, I know how I would do it if I were a devious twister like Eusebius Beck, Inspector Grant,' Jarrett said, evidently quite pleased with himself. 'What mode of conveyance is most commonly seen and heard during the twilight hours?'

'Hansoms, sir?'

'No, wheelbarrows. It is known as the 'Moonlight Flit', is it not? A husband and wife, having built up a fair stock of back rent and now facing the prospect of the Sheriff's officers seizing their few worldly goods, pile their bits and pieces on a wheelbarrow and scurry off through the night to some other lodgings, where the whole sorry business will start all over again.'

Charlie Grant nodded his agreement with this and glanced at Tommy Quinn to see if it was unanimous.

'Didn't you say that the caretaker in the Corinthian Halls put out the gas lights at eight o'clock, Inspector?' Sergeant Quinn asked.

'Then it must have been at his lodgings,' the inspector said.

Superintendent Jarrett thought this over.

'Who searched Beck's digs?'

Grant and Quinn exchanged concerned looks.

'Nobody,' Charlie Grant admitted. 'We got sidetracked, sir.'

'Then get someone over to Fiddlers Close right away. Better late than never, I suppose. In fact, Sergeant Quinn, take Williamson and a uniformed officer and obtain permission from Beck himself for a search. He won't insist on a warrant. That much you can take as read.' After Tommy Quinn had departed, Jarrett continued, 'It is certainly not outwith the realms of possibility that Miss Moffat set off the following morning to buy another pair of scissors, Inspector. But she wouldn't go back to Murray's. The question is, Inspector, can we afford to put our hard-pressed DCs onto scouring every ironmonger, hardware shop and drysalter in the city in the hope that somebody remembers a woman buying a pair of scissors? Especially if she happened to be veiled.'

'Even if some salesman did remember her,' Grant offered, 'it wouldn't prove anything. She could say she lost them. Left them on the omnibus, perhaps. My own view is that it would be a very long way from the 'beyond reasonable doubt' that the law requires.'

'Agreed,' Jarrett said. 'There is not a shred of proof, and I can't see a confession being forthcoming, but something deep down tells me she did it. I don't care about her convenient receipts. As far as I am concerned she stabbed Vincent Gittens, but whether we will ever get a conviction is quite another matter.'

★ ★ ★

George Stanton had worked for Allan and Sharpe, Builders, on Canal Street for over forty years, man and boy, and now that his useful grafting days were over they had very generously kept him on as general dogsbody, for which he was eternally grateful. And the title of Yard Supervisor more than made up for the fact that they had cut his money in half.

In his time George had seen most things and virtually every kind of falling and crushing accident, but he had never seen a man with his throat cut from ear to ear before. So there he stood, just staring at the corpse on the sand heap, taking in the large, unseeing eyes, the widely spread arms and the legs that were half-buried in the soft material. When it did finally sink in that this was neither an apprentice's trick nor a drunk dossing down behind the high wall, he turned on his heels and made for the sliding door in the hope that there might just be a copper out there.

★   ★   ★

This time it was only Superintendent Jarrett and Inspector Grant who met Dr Hamilton in the yard of the Allan and Sharpe store, since Sergeant Quinn and his men had already set off for Professor Eusebius Beck's digs before the beat constable's urgent report to his sergeant reached Davie Black at the desk and he, in turn, entirely ruined the Detective Department's morning with the unwelcome news that they had another one.

Sending an electric telegraph message to Chief Constable Rattray would have served no useful purpose, at least until the preliminary investigation of the find site had been completed. It was Inspector Grant's considered opinion that it would be time enough to interrupt his well-deserved break at his estate at Langbank when his expertise was required. But Charlie Grant wasn't fooling anyone.

For once, the find spot and the scene of the

murder were one and the same. It was Dr Hamilton's immediate and well-supported observation that the victim had been held down by at least one person while his throat was cut, and this was borne out, not only by the amount of blood, but also by the bruises on the wrists and the deep indents on either side of the body which had been caused by someone kneeling in the soft sand. That the dead man had put up a good deal of resistance was clear from the way his writhing had resulted in his feet and lower legs being almost entirely buried. Other indents, again the result of kneeling, were plainly evident close to the head.

'At least one individual pinned him down,' Hamilton said. 'The actual killer knelt at the head, but because their prey was lying it wasn't possible to pull his head back to cut his throat. So this time the cut was downwards and across, making it a more horizontal wound, as opposed to the curved ear-to-ear gash of the other two.'

'Any tattoos?'

'Inspired guess, Superintendent.' Dr Hamilton pushed the man's coat sleeve up to reveal the Red Lion on the Saltire. 'Sapper.'

'What about his identity?' Jarrett asked.

'No idea. The pockets are empty, and as you can see, Superintendent, the lining of the trouser pockets has been turned inside out.'

Henry Jarrett turned his attention to the churned sand close to the wall just a few feet from where the body was found.

'Constable,' he said and a young uniformed officer was suddenly alert and raring to go, 'take a look in the alleyway. Tell me how they got in.'

Ronald Sharpe was the sole surviving partner these twenty years. Because it would not be a demonstration of due deference to interview George Stanton ahead of his boss, Inspector Grant invited Sharpe over for a talk that both he and Jarrett knew would be absolutely fruitless.

'Have you ever seen this man before, Mr Sharpe?' Henry Jarrett asked.

'No, never.' The boss was no longer young, yet his experiences had been limited and did not include bloody murder. He grimaced and turned quickly away. 'God knows who he is, or was. He certainly didn't work for me.'

At that point the young constable returned and Jarrett withdrew a short way away, out of earshot of any curious parties.

'There are two barrels and a pile of boxes in the alley, sir' the officer said. 'You could be up and over in seconds.'

'Could you?' The superintendent nodded appreciatively. 'Then do it.'

'Sir?'

'Do it, Constable.'

Henry Jarrett then returned to the sand heap and asked, 'Do you hire a night watchman, Mr Sharpe?'

'No need. Really. I lock the main padlock when I leave at night and the beat officer is never far away.'

At that moment the young constable heaved himself up onto the wall, but moved along a few feet before dropping into the yard so that he would not disturb Dr Hamilton's nice little collection of boot prints.

'I would say you were asking for trouble leaving a pile of barrels and crates out there,' the superintendent stated, then turned to the young officer. 'How are you going to get back out, Constable?'

The boy looked around, then made directly for the Yard Superintendent's hut in the corner by the main doors. One boot on the chunky door knob, another on the low roof and he was up on the wall.

'This is one way, Superintendent,' he called. 'I can think of others.'

'No need. You can come back down.'

Since Ronald Sharpe had nothing worthwhile to contribute there was little point in detaining him further, so he was sent about his business.

'As I see it,' Jarrett said to Charlie Grant and Dr Hamilton, 'this one was probably being taken to wherever it is they kill them, but may have broken away and was chased to this spot.'

'That would certainly explain the change in the method of killing,' Dr Hamilton said. 'The cut is much less controlled.'

'But still the same weapon?'

'Oh, no doubt about that. I am still of the opinion that it is a single claw from a big cat affixed in some way to a hilt.'

'Bloody tribal, if you ask me,' Charlie Grant put in. 'What the hell does it mean?'

'I dare say it will all come out in the proverbial wash,' Jarrett said. 'But in the meantime we have to get to the basic facts of it all.'

George Stanton probably knew more about the running of the yard than anyone else. He may have sunk to the lowest place in the pecking order, but it was often the case that such a lowly individual was the lynchpin of an organization.

'As you can see,' he told Jarrett, 'the sand level is right down. Normally it would be halfway up the wall, and your dead man would be leaning against it instead of lying down.'

'Why is it so low?'

'A big job on at Tod and MacGregor's shipyard, so we are taking deliveries of materials every day at the moment.'

'That being the case,' the superintendent said, 'I would like you to take the inspector and me through an account of the daily activities in the yard.'

'Well, sir, we have one flatbed wagon for bricks and two box wagons for sand, cement and the tools. I make sure that they are all loaded and covered with tarpaulins in the evening before we close up. That way they can be rolling out of the place at first light. If we let them load up in the morning, half the forenoon would be lost. Anyway, the wagons come back and forth all day to pick up fresh supplies, which keeps the labourers in the yard busy.'

'What are the business hours?'

'I open up at six-thirty and am still here when Mr Sharpe does the honours and locks the padlock at eight-thirty.'

'Long day,' Jarrett observed.

'Perhaps, sir, but it's my life and I wouldn't trade it for anything else.'

'Lucky man,' said Charlie Grant. 'You take a quick turn around the yard before closing, I suppose?'

'Without fail.'

'And first thing in the morning?'

George gave his thinning scalp a good scratching and grinned sheepishly.

'Not always,' he admitted. 'I usually have a quick brew-up before the first of the men arrive, and it can be a bit nippy about then.'

'So when do you take a tour of your estate, Mr Stanton?'

'After the wagons have gone.' George adopted a somewhat concerned expression. 'As long as the office has not been entered and the vehicles are intact, that is all I am concerned about. I hope you won't mention this to a certain party.'

'Have no fear, Mr Stanton,' Jarrett said to put his mind at ease. 'Tell me, where are the horses kept?'

'Next door in McCandlish's Carriage Hire. Mr Sharpe pays to have them properly stabled and cared for. It works out cheaper than employing someone to do it. And anyway, there would have to be a night watchman, so that would be an added cost. He's no fool, our Mr Sharpe.'

At that moment the arrival of the blood wagon was announced by the grinding of iron-rimmed wheels and clanking hooves on the cobblestones. Dr Hamilton indicated to the driver to wheel around in the yard.

'See me this afternoon, Superintendent,' he

said. 'It is unlikely that I will be able to assist in your identification of the body, but there might be something of interest.'

★   ★   ★

Mrs Maitland's demand for block ice was seasonal, subject to the climate on any particular day, and dependent upon what she had to keep fresh. Yet Jocky Milne faithfully turned up with his cart at the front gate of 76 Delmont Avenue every day between the start of May and the end of September, then waited four or five minutes to see if anyone waved their feather dusters at him, either from this property or any of the surrounding ones. Exactly what they did at the cold factory in the Old Wynd for the remainder of the year was something of a mystery, but not one that Elsie Maitland was willing to dwell upon. Nor did she encourage Lizzie or Jeannie to do so either.

Jeannie waited by the raised flap of the wooden ice box while Jocky heaved the second clamped block into a compartment that was perfectly made for it. It was only when he had collected his fourpence and taken his leave that she giggled and caused Lizzie to follow suit without quite realising why.

'Well, there's a turn up,' she said softly in

case Mrs Maitland overheard. 'Jocky goes to Professor Beck's improvement class. He has been bettering himself for a couple of months now.'

'I thought it was only for women,' Lizzie offered.

'No, of course it isn't, but I think it's mainly young women who go. Anyway, he's going to meet me there and see me safely home.'

'Better not let Mrs Maitland know that,' Lizzie cautioned. 'No followers or fanciers, you know.'

'He's not a follower,' Jeannie said. 'Not yet, anyway.'

'My, you get ahead of yourself, Jeannie Craig.'

'Oh, I don't think so. He isn't just a carter, you know. It's his family that owns the works, so I could do a lot worse than him.'

'Why can't you just settle for what you've got?' Lizzie admonished, but even as she said it she knew how foolish it sounded. They all dreamt about changing places with the lady of the house, and Elsie Maitland was living proof that it could be done. 'You've got a nice home here. What more do you want?'

Jeannie stared at her as though she had taken leave of her senses.

'You're pulling my leg, aren't you?' she said with a grin.

'Sort of,' Lizzie admitted, 'but you could do a lot worse than what you've got.'

'And a lot better. Just give me the chance and I'll show you what I can do.'

'Maybe that's what Jocky Milne's thinking,' said Lizzie with a chuckle. 'I don't believe for a minute that he's ever been to the class. I'll bet he only said that after you told him about it.'

'No, he didn't.'

'Are you telling me you didn't show him that newspaper cutting first?'

Jeannie frowned.

'Yes, but that was when he told me he knew all about it. If I hadn't shown the paper the subject would never have been mentioned. It must have been fate, you see, or the power of thought. It sometimes works.'

'Yes, and that's what Mrs Maitland will be thinking about you if you don't prepare the vegetables.'

* * *

Tommy Quinn's visit to Eusebius Beck's lodgings in Fiddlers Close had turned out to be a great deal less than profitable. Beck offered no resistance to an unwarranted search of his two-room diggings and even went out of his way to be helpful. It was plain from the first moment that they were going to find nothing, and certainly not a speck of blood or any other indication that Vincent Gittens died there.

Nor was there any sign of a push barrow in the narrow alleys that surrounded the old building. Of course, that mode of transportation of the body was entirely hypothetical, but remained nevertheless the most likely method. And Amelia Moffat remained the most likely suspect.

'There was nothing, Superintendent,' Sergeant Quinn stated when he returned to headquarters. 'To be honest, I didn't think there would be. The place has been scrubbed from top to bottom, so whatever else Miss Moffat might be she is not a slattern.'

'Pity,' Jarrett said, but he was clearly not expecting any other result. 'Anyway, it kept you away from the fun.'

'Bad, sir?'

'Very messy. There's a lot of blood in the human body, Sergeant.'

'Which would suggest that the one holding the victim down was probably drenched,' Charlie Grant observed.

'I think we can safely assume that to be the case.' Jarrett paused and conjured up the image of a blood-man with soaked clothing and a smeared face. 'It wouldn't be possible for anyone to walk through the streets in that condition, whatever time of day or night it was.'

'A carriage,' Tommy Quinn suggested.

'Private. A Hansom would have been out of the question. Most of the drivers won't pick up a drunk, let alone someone in that state.'

'It all points to a rushed job,' Charlie Grant said. 'You are probably right about the chase, Superintendent. By the looks of things it was not how it was meant to be.'

'No, and they're not finished yet. If our original guess is correct, there is one more member of the gang still at risk.'

'Unless he's the one carrying out the slaughter of his compatriots,' Tommy Quinn said.

'That doesn't feel right. So far, I think we can safely say that we have accumulated the earthly remains of the leader and two of his diggers. That would suggest that the still surviving member of the team is a digger, but so far the two sappers on Dr Hamilton's tables don't give me the impression of having either the resources or the organizational skills to carry out a series of such assassinations.'

'Also, we now know that there are two killers,' Inspector Grant offered. 'Or at least a killer and his accomplice.'

'But we can't even begin to understand

what it is all about.'

'No,' Grant agreed, 'but I still don't think it's British. It's worse than tribal. It's bloody barbaric.'

'Yes, I know what you mean.' Jarrett looked from one to the other as he sought clarification from somewhere, anywhere. 'Let us hope Dr Hamilton can shed at least a glimmer of light before this day turns into a complete disaster.'

★　★　★

'What do you make of that, Superintendent?' Hamilton asked, placing the brass disk on the table and watching while each of them examined it in turn. It was a little over an inch in diameter, quite thin and stamped only on one side. 'CH 127. It was inside his boot and probably the only possession he had in the world that was worth protecting.'

'It looks like a brothel token,' Charlie Grant suggested.

'I will take your word for that,' Dr Hamilton said. 'But you are on the right track, even if the truth is a little less exotic. It is, in fact, a token for the Charity Hostel and guarantees a needy man a place to sleep and a meal.'

Jarrett passed the object to Tommy Quinn

and said, 'If he and Neil Goudie were in on it with Hadden why were they totally devoid of funds? How can a man who has just carried out a bank robbery be in the Charity Hostel? Have we got it wrong?'

'I don't think so,' Inspector Grant said. 'No other explanation makes sense. Christopher Hadden supervised the digging of the tunnel by Neil Goudie and this individual at least, and possibly one other.'

'You are still adhering to that as the way of things?'

'Indeed I am, sir.'

'Then we must locate the last man before it is too late, gentlemen.'

'Any thoughts on how that might be done, Superintendent?' Tommy Quinn enquired.

'It can only be by poster, and let us thank God the CC isn't here or he would almost certainly ignite.' Jarrett collected his thoughts. 'I want you to see to it, Sergeant Quinn. There must be no mention of the bank robbery, but make it clear that anyone who has recently associated with Christopher Hadden and Neil Goudie, among others, stands in mortal danger and must contact us immediately. Make sure they go up in every post office, pub and doss house in the city.'

'Can we offer immunity from prosecution

as an incentive, Superintendent?'

'We can't do that. Suggest some sort of deal if you wish, but keep it vague. The important thing is to scare him into seeking our protection.'

★ ★ ★

Charlie Grant thought it best to arrive at the Charity Hostel on foot rather than by wagonette. That would not have been the best way to ingratiate himself with the regulars.

Not that there was even the remotest possibility of concealing his profession from the unfortunates who lay, or sat on the narrow cots. There was no need to introduce himself or display the badge, because few among them had not been in trouble many times and knew the stink of the law only too well. Even when he explained that he was trying to identify one of their number he wasn't believed. They thought that he was lying in order to break an alibi or in some other way obtain a conviction.

Until he came to Billy Strang, that is.

'Where did you get it?' he asked, when Grant showed him the brass disk.

'It was in his boot. He's dead.'

Billy nodded sadly as he rummaged around in what was left of his jacket for one of the

219

cheroot butts he had rescued from the pavement.

'How'd he die?' he asked.

'Does it matter?'

'We were pals, Eddie White and me. India, Africa, elsewhere.' Billy pushed his left sleeve up. There was no shirt. His ingrained forearm carried the tattoo of the now familiar red lion on a blue and white Saltire. 'We used to talk a lot about how we'd cop it.'

'He was murdered.'

'Jesus! Why the hell would anyone murder Eddie? He hadn't a bloody bean.'

'That might not have been the reason.'

'What then?' Billy stared at the inspector and tried to make sense of this information. 'I suppose we always thought it would come violently, from a wild man's spear or a knobkerrie or even a hill fighter's rifle, but that was war we were talking about. This is meant to be peace.'

'We think he got in with a bad crowd.'

'Never. He would have told me.'

Charlie Grant gave this some thought, then asked, 'Were you and Eddie White involved in any bad business lately?'

'What sort of bad business? Do you mean thieving? If I had come into a bit of cash do you think I'd be sitting in this flea pit? Have a bit of sense, Inspector.'

But that sort of argument had no effect on an inspector with his length of service. Smart robbers didn't flash their newfound wealth; they squirreled it and waited until the hue and cry had died away.

'I'm going to have to take you in, Billy,' Grant said. 'Maybe you'll have a sudden attack of memory when you're in the interview room.'

'Now, wait a minute.' Strang raised both palms to indicate parley. 'The charity people are strict, you know. You have to sing your hymns and eat your grub without complaint, and if you get into trouble you are out on your arse. If I'm seen being led away that's it as far as I'm concerned.'

'Then tell me what you know, Billy.'

'But I don't know anything. Eddie and I did our service together and went the way of old soldiers, but neither of us has been involved with the law for some time now. This isn't much of a billet, but it's a damned sight better than the park or a doorway.'

Charlie Grant produced his restrainers and dangled them in front of Strang's eyes.

'Last chance, Billy,' he said flatly. 'Either you talk here or you talk at Central.'

For a few moments the former soldier sat in silence and watched the swinging cuffs.

'Right,' he said, 'I'll tell you all I know,

which isn't much, but I want you to promise me you'll leave me out of it.'

'That depends on what you've done, Billy. Some things I can overlook and some things I can't.'

'I wasn't involved, so there's nothing to do me for.'

'Involved in what?'

'Whatever it was.'

Inspector Grant's patience was not inexhaustible, and now it had reached its limit. He placed a hand on Strang's shoulder.

'Come on,' he said firmly. 'I've had about enough of this.'

'No, wait a minute.' Billy had realized that he had run out of time and bluffing would not work. 'I don't know for certain what it was, but Eddie told me he had been offered the chance to do a bit of digging with no questions asked.'

'What kind of digging?'

'That's the point, Inspector. I don't know and I don't think he did either.'

'Are you trying to say that Eddie White was involved in a crime without knowing anything about it?'

'That's exactly what I'm saying. He had been approached by an officer from the old days and offered one hundred pounds for one night's tunnelling. It doesn't take a genius to see that it was illegal, but no details were gone into.'

'You must know where it was,' Grant stated.

'I do now, but even Eddie had no idea at the time. All he knew was that he and a couple of others from the regiment were to be taken somewhere to do a particular job. When he came back he told me it was a bank.'

'Why weren't you offered the chance to make a hundred?'

'I can't dig now, that's why. I've got a rheumy elbow from sleeping rough.'

'So what happened to the money he was paid?'

'I don't think he got it. The officer told them that he didn't want them showing off until he was well away, so they were going to get their portion in a week or so.'

'And they agreed to that?' Grant said, grinning. 'You must think I'm an idiot, Billy.'

'But it's true. He explained that the sort of things he was after they could do nothing with. If a scruff tried to pawn anything that sparkled he'd be lifted right away. They agreed, because all they wanted was cash, not bloody jewellery and that sort of stuff.'

'All right,' the inspector said, hesitatingly, 'We'll pretend I'm daft and that I believe you. Who was in it with him?'

'Captain Hadden. He was in charge.'

'And the others?'

'I don't know. Eddie only mentioned Hadden.'

'So it was Hadden, Eddie White and two others. Is that it?'

'That's what he told me, Inspector. Honest to God.'

★ ★ ★

Since no image was available, and therefore no engraving required, Tommy Quinn collected five hundred handbills just before three o'clock that afternoon and issued instructions that all had to be on display before the day was out. The combination chosen by Superintendent Jarrett himself was bold black on yellow paper, which was nature's own warning sign. After that it was just a matter of hoping that the last man, if indeed he existed at all, caught sight of a flier before the killers caught sight of him.

'I think we can be fairly sure he's out there,' Jarrett said when Grant and Quinn had both joined him in the office. 'If this Billy Strang character is telling the truth, we can only hope that the third man sees one of Sergeant Quinn's posters in time.'

'He might be dead already,' Charlie Grant stated. 'Just because he hasn't come to our attention doesn't mean he's still kicking.'

11

Superintendent Henry Jarrett spent all of the previous evening and much of the night trying to make sense of Vincent Gittens's notes, and somehow link them to what they had found. By the time he reached the office the following morning he was really none the wiser.

'Too many lions, gentlemen, too much of a coincidence altogether.'

'Two tattoos and Cyrus Brand's brooch?' Tommy Quinn said quizzically.

'And a murder device that is almost certainly the claw of a big cat set into a handle. Not to mention our third digger, should he exist and should we find him. If he doesn't have a lion on his arm I'll be very much surprised.'

Charlie Grant appreciated this and observed, 'The tattoos and the brooch I can understand, but the throat-ripper is quite another matter. Every time I tell myself that it is not British I find that I am more and more convinced of this.'

'Not British in the normal course of things, perhaps,' Jarrett replied, 'but what if it was a dreadful penalty attached to a secret society? Prominent societies have blood-curdling punishments for treason built into their oaths of allegiance.'

'Yes, but they don't actually carry them out. I have never heard of anyone having, quote, '*my body severed in two, my bowels taken from thence and burned to ashes*'. Yet countless decent citizens have agreed to that penalty.'

'Granted, Superintendent, but perhaps not all societies are peopled by responsible and law-abiding men. Some who gravitate to clandestine groups are not what you and I would consider to be normal.'

Even as he found himself agreeing with Charlie Grant's view of such things, Henry Jarrett's mind was drifting back to the previous evening, when he had come to a very similar conclusion.

He had devoted a considerable amount of time after dinner to trying to make sense of Vincent Gittens's most recent jottings, which were typical of someone who could think quicker that he could scribble. The result was a jumble of miscellaneous sentences and bits of undeveloped ideas that would probably have meant something to him in the short term, but could swiftly fade into a confusing mish-mash of woolly thoughts. A good speed-writing technique would have been infinitely better, but Jarrett suspected that Gittens was probably too impatient to learn such a thing.

There was no doubt, however, that the man had been getting about and garnering snippets wherever he could. Tracking down these sources and squeezing a bit more out of them would not be a simple task, but it had to be done.

After studying the book in front of his Wardian case for some time and getting nowhere, the superintendent had crossed to the bed where he lay back and scanned the words repeatedly until he found himself putting together a picture that was very possibly as far from the truth as could be. Yet if Gittens's words were to be taken at face value there was no other apparent conclusion to be reached.

Abyss. Abyss = pit? Lion pit? Edin and Stir lion pits. Lion Rampant. Lion of the Abyss? Gold lion. Abyss gold. Gold of the Abyss? Murch GU. What is this? Secret Society? What did Hadden know? Was he one of them, or did he find out too much?

Jarrett produced Gittens's notebook and

read aloud the jottings while Inspector Grant and Sergeant Quinn silently took in every word.

'Well, gentlemen,' he said at length, 'what do we make of that?'

'What is Murch GU?' Tommy Quinn asked.

'I can't say off hand,' the superintendent confessed, 'but if you would care to visit the Glasgow University you might find out.'

Charlie Grant cocked an eye at his boss as he scratched his jaw in that knowing way of his.

'Would you like me to tell you a story we got at school?' he asked.

'Proceed, Inspector. We are agog.'

'Well, sir, it's about Mary Queen of Scots. Apparently she was born in Linlithgow Palace and when she was a little girl her nurse, Janet Sinclair, would take her to the lion pit to throw titbits to the beasts.'

'That's most interesting, Inspector,' Jarrett said, but he meant it this time and there was no trace of mockery in his tone. 'That could very well be the seed from which some wild association has since grown.'

★   ★   ★

Dr Murchison drew open the door and welcomed Tommy Quinn to his study, which overlooked the hustle and bustle of High Street.

'To be honest, Sergeant,' he said, 'there isn't a great deal of good, solid material pertaining to the keeping of big cats. If you believe the legends, and a few untrustworthy writings, it would seem that in bygone days the kings kept African lions in the same way that we might keep songbirds or rabbits. Certainly, there is a ten-foot deep circular pit at Linlithgow Palace, between the great hall and the woods, which is believed to have been a lions' den in the time of Queen Mary. And there are also reputed lion pits in Edinburgh and Stirling castles, and very probably every other castle as well. And why not? Keeping such beasts would only have reflected the cruel and vengeful nature of the times.'

'Would they just have been pets, or do you think there was something murderous behind keeping these animals?'

'Oh, I don't think so. It wasn't a Roman amphitheatre, you know, although I wouldn't be a bit surprised to learn that someone had met a grisly end in one of those pits. There were some particularly horrible characters back then.'

'There are some pretty horrible characters now.'

'Yes, Sergeant, but at least you are here to protect us.'

Not quite sure how to take that, Tommy Quinn checked the notes he had prepared, to make sure that he had covered all the points.

'The image of a standing lion,' he began, 'presumably has some connection with these creatures, Dr Murchison.'

'Not as you perhaps mean it. Correct me if I'm wrong, but you are probably assuming that the Lion Rampant image was adopted as a result of the early kings' penchant for the beasts. In fact, that is only partly right. If you accept Campion's Histories, this tropical beast, as he names it, came to be the Blazon of Scotland when the first kings arrived from your native land, Sergeant Quinn. They brought with them a marble throne and the image of a lion, both of which had talismanic qualities. Yet the lion is no more a native of Ireland than of Scotland, so it has long been believed that the throne and the image were introduced into Ireland by the Prophet Jeremiah, and from there they were subsequently taken to Scotland. The marble seat, it seems, was the Throne of King David and the Lion Rampant was the Ensign of the Tribe of Judah. In Christianity, Sergeant Quinn, the lion is often taken to be another name for Jesus. It is a very important image in several countries, including Abyssinia.'

Tommy Quinn glanced again at his notes, but this time his attention affixed itself to just one word — Abyss.

'Tell me,' he asked, 'would you say that abyss was a good synonym for pit?'

'No, I wouldn't say so. Abyss suggests a void or chasm, or a bottomless pit, perhaps, but somehow pit alone isn't quite adequate.'

'So 'Lion of the Abyss' is meaningless?'

'It has meaning if it refers to the Lion of the Abyssinians.'

'And Abyss gold? Would that be Abyssinian gold?'

'I hope not.' Murchison laughed then, and snatched up a well-worn dictionary. 'If I might check my facts. Yes, here we are. Abyssinian gold has very little to do with Abyssinia, and even less to do with gold. It is, in fact, an alloy of copper and zinc, which is used to make mock gold for ladies who cannot afford quantities of the real thing. It is apparently very difficult to spot when it is being worn, since it cannot be tested for weight.'

'Somehow, I don't think that applies to the object I have in mind.'

'I am very pleased to hear it.' Dr Murchison laid his dictionary on the desk and reached instead for his rather dishevelled copy of *The Times* and thumbed through it until he found what he was looking for. He handed it to Quinn. 'Quite topical, Sergeant. A few months ago, King Theodore II of Abyssinia made an appeal to Britain to assist him in his war against his non-Christian neighbours. Gladstone, however, has been reluctant to become embroiled in foreign adventures. Just another reason for the Abyssinians to be displeased with us.'

Tommy Quinn read and re-read the article, but although it seemed that it should be relevant, it did not immediately strike him as such. Unless, of course, Vincent Gittens had also been looking into this story. But the *Advertiser* was a local rag with little or no interest in international affairs, unless there was some direct connection to Glasgow.

'I'm sorry — ' he began.

'The missing *tabots?*' Murchison leaned forward and peered at him. 'The Ark of the Covenant?'

'Forgive me, Dr Murchison, but — '

'No, I am the one who should apologize, Sergeant Quinn. I tend to assume that everyone takes an interest in such matters.' Murchison accepted the return of *The Times* and sat back as he invariably did when preparing to launch into a lecture. 'Another legend, this time from long, long ago.'

'Menelik, son of King Solomon, is reputed to have removed the Ark, with its Commandments, from the Temple of Jerusalem and transported it to the land of his mother, the Queen of Sheba. Today we call this Aksum in northern Abyssinia. While a final resting place was being prepared for it, the Ark rested on two planks of acacia wood. These strips were later cut into squares and carved with Biblical scenes, making them the first *tabots*, or sacred icons. The most important of these by far were the four on which the corners of the Ark had rested, for they were thought to have been touched by God.'

'Now we leap forward many centuries, to a point just about five years ago. An explorer passing through Abyssinia was shown the holiest *tabots*, but when he had gone it was discovered that they were missing, along with a gold lion brooch used to hold the high priest's cloak together and a claw weapon carried by this man. The explorer, or whatever he really was, had apparently chosen his moment well, because it was the time of the great rains which eventually flood the Nile valley and without which Egypt would die. If he had waited a day or so he would have been trapped, but he escaped ahead of the flood which made it impossible for them to follow him. To this day, Sergeant, King

233

Theodore II has agents scouring the world in search of the thief and the holy relics. Their orders are to return God's treasures to Aksum.'

And that, Tommy Quinn thought as he closed his notebook, was going to make Superintendent Jarrett's day.

★   ★   ★

It wasn't often that Davie Black left his desk at the main foyer to another, lesser mortal, but on this occasion his news was so urgent that it would be quicker to deliver it himself than relate it to a constable, who would almost certainly get it wrong.

Henry Jarrett stopped talking abruptly and both he and Charlie Grant turned in the direction of the cheery face that was beaming at them from around the partly opened door.

'Ran in all of a lather and said he wanted to talk to the head man,' Sergeant Black said. 'I've got young Chapman keeping an eye on him in case he tries to trot.'

'Who exactly are we holding, Sergeant Black?' Jarrett asked.

Davie held up the wrinkled yellow poster their guest had used to introduce himself.

'Him,' he said.

When he saw the two officers approaching

him along the narrow hallway, the man rose from the slatted seat and looked dead set to bolt, but PC Chapman laid a hand on his shoulder and made sure this never came to pass.

'Let me see your left arm,' Superintendent Jarrett stated.

It may have been an unusual form of introduction, but the stranger was used to taking orders and obliged by shrugging off his jacket. He pushed up an uncuffed shirt sleeve, exposing the anticipated lion on the diagonal cross.

'Thank you,' Jarrett said. 'I just wanted to make sure you weren't seeking a cell to doss in. We get several of them every day.'

When they reached the interrogation room, the former soldier identified himself as Gilbert Purvis, unmarried, living alone in a single-room dwelling above the bazaar in the Candleriggs, and earning a living as a porter in the fruit and vegetable market. He hadn't noticed the poster in Wiley's Bar until late the previous night, but by then he was too unsteady on his feet to want to attract the attention of the law.

'The story in your own words,' Jarrett said, then he and Charlie Grant sat back with their arms folded to listen and, hopefully, learn something. 'Any questions can wait.'

'Am I facing prosecution?'

'Yes, you are, but whatever help you give us will be explained to the court. Do you have a criminal record?'

'No, sir. I've never been charged with anything.'

'Then you should be treated leniently, Mr Purvis. Now, your story, if you please.'

The man made something of a show of marshalling his thoughts.

'An officer from my old regiment, Captain Hadden, had been making enquiries about me in the market. Then one day he was waiting at the top of the stairs when I got home. You don't argue with officers, even after your service, so I took him in and waited while he told me his plan.

'For reasons that were none of my business, me and a couple of others were being offered a night's digging for a hundred sovereigns apiece. There was no mention of a bank, or I wouldn't have had anything to do with it. I want you to know that.

'Anyway, the four of us met up in Sammy's Chop House in Argyle Street and Captain Hadden told us that we had to be able to put aside the following Saturday night. As I said, we were to get one hundred each, but only after a week or so because he thought we would go on the flash and play at silly

236

buggers. Him being an officer, we just accepted that and didn't argue.

'So, early on the Saturday evening we three diggers made our way to the shop on Byres Road. The street was still busy, so no one paid any attention to us. A good organizer, Captain Hadden, I'll say that for him. All the gear we needed was waiting for us, along with a good basket of ham, cheese and bread, and plenty of water. No booze, he said. It dehydrates you and makes you loud into the bargain. So we hung black curtains over the window and door, and another one across the middle of the shop just to be doubly sure. While the three of us dug, cleared and stacked, Captain Hadden positioned himself in the front shop to take care of any problems that could arise. If the local bobby had rattled the door he wouldn't have doubted a gent, would he?'

When Purvis fell silent, Superintendent Jarrett said, 'You know Hadden is dead, don't you? So are Neil Goudie and Eddie White. You are the last of them.'

Gilbert Purvis stared at him for a long time. At first it was clear that he thought they were joking, perhaps trying to fool him into saying something that might incriminate him even more, but it soon became apparent that this was not so.

237

'But how?' he breathed. 'There was nothing said about that on the poster.'

'Of course not, but you must have realized that something was wrong when you were warned to contact us for your own safety.'

'Yes, but I couldn't understand why. All I knew was that it frightened the hell out of me. I had to think a long time before coming in here, because I was pretty sure it was a trick.'

'Well, now you know otherwise. All we wanted to do was save your life, Mr Purvis.'

'I appreciate that.' Purvis gave an easy gesture. 'We weren't friends, you know. We were all sappers, but we didn't know each other that well.'

'Did you know Billy Strang?' Inspector Grant asked.

'I knew him, but he palled around with Eddie White.'

'Was Strang in on the robbery?'

'No, he had nothing to do with it.' Purvis paused briefly. 'I want you to know that we weren't told anything about a robbery.'

'You must have known that you weren't planting flowers.'

'Of course, but there was never any mention of breaking into a bank, or breaking into anything, for that matter. It wasn't until we came up through the floor that we had some idea what it was all about. But by then it was too late to back out. We'd done it and that was an end of it.'

'The boxes,' Jarrett said flatly. 'Who burst them open?'

'We all did. Captain Hadden told me and Eddie to take the forty on one side, while he and Neil Goudie took the other side.'

'Do you know what Hadden was after?'

'Nothing in particular, I don't think. He just told us to ignore papers and the like, but let him know if we came across anything of value.'

'And did you?'

'A few bits of jewellery and gold coins.'

Henry Jarrett stared into the man's eyes. Seeking out the slightest wavering that would indicate evasion.

'A gold lion brooch or badge,' he said. 'Did you find it?'

'Yes, that was one of my finds.'

'Can you remember what else was in that particular box?'

'Not really. A few bits of wood wrapped up in a big hanky thing, and some documents, but I really can't remember that well. There was a lot of boxes to get through.'

Jarrett glanced at Charlie Grant. They were both thinking the same thing.

'What did you take for yourself, Mr

Purvis?' the superintendent asked.

'Nothing.' The old soldier looked suddenly offended. 'The arrangement was one hundred each. What could we do with valuables in our condition? You lot would have had us right away.'

'That is sense talking, but in the heat of the moment sense does not have a great deal to do with it.' Jarrett continued to study the man and could see that he had hit a nerve. 'What did you pocket?'

'Nothing.' Purvis looked even more crestfallen, but his eyes revealed the anger of a frustrated man who was forbidden by rank to defend himself. 'All right, Captain Hadden saw me sticking a brooch into my shirt pocket and told me to put it back in the kitty. He had a large cloth laid out on the floor for any valuables and that was to be his portion.'

'Didn't you think it was being divided unfairly?'

'I suppose we did, but how did we know what something was worth? Anyway, cash suited us best. No difficulties with that.'

'Then why did you try to make away with the brooch?'

'I don't know. Just one of those things, I suppose. Saw an opportunity and chanced my arm.'

'Do you know if any of the others took anything?'

'I don't think so. Captain Hadden was everywhere, watching everything.'

'Well, you have been very cooperative, Mr Purvis,' Jarrett admitted, 'and this will greatly assist you when it comes to court. If you can think of anything else, that would also act in your favour.'

Gilbert Purvis thought long and hard.

'Captain Hadden never seemed to be one for the ladies,' he said eventually, 'so something he said made me wonder. I don't know if any of the others noticed it, because we didn't meet up again until a week later in Sammy's Chop House, and by then I'd forgotten it. We were too concerned at not getting paid, I suppose.'

'What exactly did he say?'

'Well, he picked up the gold lion and seemed to know what it was. Then he said, 'Ugly object, but they think it is beautiful', and laughed as though it was some kind of great big joke.'

'But he didn't say who 'they' were?'

'No, that was all. He was just talking to himself, I suppose.'

'No doubt he was, Mr Purvis,' Jarrett said. 'Meanwhile, I strongly recommend that you do not apply for bail. There is every reason to believe that those who killed your cohorts already know who you are and where you live.'

★ ★ ★

Jeannie Craig was mad and getting madder by the minute. Jocky Milne might not be much of a catch, but he was the first click she had had in months and now he had left her standing outside the Corinthian Halls. She waited until she could hear the piano then went in and took her place with the other self-improvers. As usual, the audience was mainly made up of young women, with a smattering of unappealing males.

When Professor Beck caused the purple-clad Miss Moffat to rise a few inches from the floor of the stage and slowly rotate until she was horizontal, Jeannie's common sense told her that it was a trick, but lurking at the back of her mind was the nagging doubt that there might be a greater power at work. But either way, this opening act alone was well worth the shilling she had paid for admission.

While waiting for Beck to put in an appearance, Jeannie had busied herself counting the number of occupied seats and reached the handsome total of thirty-two. If this was a typical audience on each of the three nights, the week's earnings amounted to four pounds and sixteen shillings, a very tidy sum indeed. Professor Eusebius Beck and his assistant thus could boast an annual income of more than two hundred and forty pounds, or twenty times the wages of a domestic such as herself.

She was still mentally juggling with this staggering revelation when she left the Corinthian Halls at eight o'clock and made her way to the horse-bus stance on Hope Street. Jocky Milne, his tousled red hair and his cheeky grin had all but faded from memory and she was no longer rehearsing the things she was going to say to him when the ice wagon called in the morning. Professor Beck's quiet voice and even, precisely-delivered phrases had calmed her down to such an extent that she was completely unaware of the one seated immediately behind her, his unblinking eyes fixed on the back of her bonnet.

The omnibus passed Wylie & Lochhead's store at eight ten, according to the large clock over the entrance, which meant that she alighted at Mountford Avenue at roughly twenty past. It would have been nice if the evening service had taken in Highfield Road, because then it would have been no distance at all down Delmont Avenue to Mrs Maitland's house, where she planned to recite the whole evening's discoveries to Lizzie Gill, whether the latter wished it or not. As it was, however, she was faced with a long walk around the new park, still in the process of creation and not yet fenced in, or a brisk, devil-may-care march along the moonlit wheelbarrow paths to the orchard at the rear of the property. Perhaps inevitably, she chose the wrong one.

It was only natural that Jeannie should glance over her shoulder, not once but many times as she strode out and made directly for the comforting lights in the middle distance. And she was experiencing a very familiar phenomenon — namely that the bus stop she had left was quickly diminishing in size while her destination did not appear to be getting much closer. Of course this made no more sense than the idea of someone gaining on her when there was never a figure in sight. Just wild fears, totally unfounded.

Then a hand was clamped over her mouth and the point of a blade touched her neck just below the right ear.

* * *

Henry Jarrett was trying to make sense of Tommy Quinn's account of his meeting with Dr Murchison when the commotion down-stairs jerked him instantly back into the here

244

and now. Yet quick as he was, James Croall and Wilbur McConnell had beaten him to the balcony and were literally hanging over the rail in their desire to learn what was going on. As he swept past them and down the stairs, Jarrett noted with interest that neither had ventured down to the lobby to find out.

'It's Jeannie,' Elsie Maitland said urgently. 'There's been an incident.'

Fortunately, Mrs Maitland had still been in the kitchen when Lizzie opened the back door to admit the girl, because the moment she entered the house Jeannie had made straight for this warm place where she felt most at home.

'Someone grabbed her, Mr Jarrett,' Lizzie said urgently when the superintendent appeared in the doorway. 'She broke away, but she's quite shaken up.'

Jarrett never found such situations easy to cope with, but at least it could have been much worse. He asked, 'Did you get a look at him, Jeannie? Or did he say anything?'

The girl shook her head.

'It was all so quick. He seized me and put a blade to my neck just here on the right side of my neck, but luckily he didn't break the skin.' She paused for a moment, before adding, 'Somehow, I wriggled free immediately and ran for it. I kept thinking he was right behind me, but he wasn't. He must have made off in a different direction.'

'Well, thank God for that.' Jarrett waited until Lizzie had poured the girl a cup of tea from the pot that seemed to be always brewing. Then he said, 'Any information will be helpful. I know it is asking a bit much, but could you even guess at his height, or age, or indeed anything?'

'No, there's nothing at all. It might have been anybody, Mr Jarrett, anybody at all.' Suddenly, a thought struck her. 'There was a strange smell on his fingers. It was neither pleasant nor unpleasant, just odd. I remember it from somewhere, but I can't think right now.'

'Could it have been greasepaint?'

'I don't really know what that smells like, sir.'

'Not to worry. It will probably come back to you. In the meantime, let us try a different approach. Did anyone know you were going to be out and about this evening?'

Jeannie looked at Lizzie then and received a nod of encouragement.

'Jocky Milne,' she whispered. 'He was to meet me there, but he never turned up.'

Mrs Maitland frowned then, since this was the first she had heard of any such liaison. But it was neither the time nor the place for recriminations.

'You had better tell Superintendent Jarrett everything, my girl,' she said, but kindly. 'How long has this been going on?'

'It hasn't, ma'am.' Faced with having broken the rule regarding followers, Jeannie hastened to explain. 'I mentioned that I was going to the improvement class and he said that he was already going there. I just thought it would be good to go inside with somebody I knew so that I didn't feel like such an outsider. I'm sorry, Mrs Maitland.'

'No need to be sorry. I know exactly what you mean.'

'This improvement class,' Jarrett enquired, 'where was it?'

'Corinthian Halls, sir. It was a Professor Beck doing it. He was very good.'

'That is not how I would describe him. Beck is many things, but good isn't one of them.' The superintendent beckoned Elsie Maitland aside and out of earshot of the girls. 'Will you be getting ice tomorrow?'

'I don't have to. I have a gigot of mutton, which keeps well and nothing else needs cooling.'

'Good, because I don't want her confronting this boy until my men have had a chance to talk to him.'

'You think he may be the one?'

'It is certainly a strong possibility,' Jarrett

admitted, 'but there is another candidate, so we must tread cautiously.'

'Well, as far as Jeannie is concerned, she won't be going anywhere for quite some time. I'll make sure of that. Lizzie will attend to all the trades people until this matter is resolved.'

12

When Sergeant Quinn had returned to headquarters after his visit to the Glasgow University the previous day, his account of his meeting with Dr Murchison enlightened and confused in equal measure. The prevalence of lion pits, and indeed the entire lion issue, certainly pointed to the possibility of a misguided cult. But if such a group had set out to finance its activities by robbing a bank, were the murders of Hadden, Goudie and White merely an exercise in cutting the chain? If so, why so barbarically, and why was Hadden tortured? For some reason he couldn't quite put his finger on, Henry Jarrett was not comfortable with the whole sect idea. There had to be another answer.

But first things first. The Jeannie Craig incident had brought the whole assault business once again to the fore, and since it had become his pet bugbear, as soon as he arrived in the office Tommy Quinn was sent to track down Jocky Milne. If that proved fruitless, he was to beard the infamous Professor Beck in his den.

'Cyrus Brand, Esquire, lied to me,' Jarrett

said firmly, when Quinn had departed. 'I think it is painfully obvious that he is the explorer who fled from Abyssinia with their sacred what-nots.'

'*Tabots*, I believe, Superintendent.'

'Quite.' In fact, Jarrett's annoyance stemmed less from the fact that Brand had adjusted the truth than from what he saw as his own stupidity. 'I actually returned the gold lion to him.'

'And you were right to do so, sir.'

'But he stole it. I gave him back an item he had purloined.'

'That's a very difficult area,' Charlie Grant said, shaking his head. 'I don't think the Fiscal is going to prosecute Brand for helping himself to some foreign artefact, any more than they condemned Elgin for rescuing the Marbles, or Monteith for relieving the maharajah of his gems. Also, as Murchison said, Gladstone isn't overly chummy with these people at the moment, so Brand has nothing to worry about and you were only doing your duty.'

'Perhaps so, Inspector, but there is something about the Brand affair that rings like a lead bell.'

'I don't see what. He still has his wooden items, the bearer bonds he showed you were safely at home, and you located the only object that had actually been taken from his box. In short he lost nothing. If you are trying to connect Cyrus Brand to the murders I don't see how you can possibly do it. He had probably less reason for killing Hadden than any of the other box holders.'

Put like that, Jarrett really had no choice but concede in good part.

'We will put Brand aside for the moment,' he suggested, 'and also put aside the notion of a secret society. We will consider instead the possibility that Hadden was tortured to make him reveal the names of the rest of the gang.'

'Why?'

'Perhaps his co-plotters thought that he had been less than honest with them. They may have expected a larger haul than they got.'

'But why kill the diggers. They were to get one hundred pounds each.'

Jarrett fell silent then and considered other alternatives.

'There is always the possibility that the murders are being carried out by professional criminals intent on getting their hands on the loot,' he said at length. 'It could be that Hadden and his amateurs had carried out a robbery that was beyond the scope of the gangs. After all, he had the shop as an entry point and a group of sappers who were experienced in tunnelling.'

'How would this criminal gang have located Hadden?' Charlie Grant asked. 'Would he be so foolish as to reveal such a thing to anyone outside the group?'

'Not intentionally, Inspector,' Superintendent Jarrett admitted. 'But who can say what a man might do under certain circumstances?'

'Such as?'

'To put it delicately, intimate.'

'You think he may have confided in a woman?'

'That is one possibility.'

'Once again, why would the killers want the names of his companions? The proceeds weren't shared out. Who would want to hunt down and brutally kill a group of hired diggers?'

'Good questions, Inspector, but sadly no real answers. So perhaps we should consider Hadden's reference to 'they', who are obviously the original owners of the piece. According to Dr Murchison, Abyssinian agents are scouring the world for the stolen items. Might they not have killed Hadden and the others?'

'Once more, Superintendent, how could they know who committed the bank robbery?

That is the question that is going to come back to haunt us every time. Whether it is a murderous gang of criminals or foreign nationals hunting down their religious items, we are always going to be faced with the problem of how they knew about Hadden. And we have to ask ourselves how it could be that these hypothetical Abyssinians knew how to find Hadden but seemingly didn't know about Cyrus Brand, the very man who in all probability stole their sacred artefacts.

'And one other point, sir. We already agreed that Hadden would not endure that sort of suffering for a gold brooch. Whatever the torturers were after it was a damned sight more important than that. Important enough for Hadden to die for.'

'Unless he didn't have the answer to whatever it was they wanted to know.'

Charlie Grant shrugged then, because they had more or less run out of ideas and not one of them showed promise.

★ ★ ★

Tommy Quinn's morning turned out to be less than successful. Jocky Milne had failed to turn up at the Corinthian Halls because he had been asked to work late at the ice plant, and could produce half a dozen workmates to vouch for that, not to mention the manager, Mr Wilkins. As for Professor Eusebius Beck, he very conveniently had one of his private consultations after the lecture, an alibi that was not only substantiated by Amelia Moffat, but also by the hall caretaker who had to remain to turn the gas off. It was simply not within the realms of possibility that either suspect could have been involved in the attack on Jeannie Craig.

With the most likely possibilities eliminated, Sergeant Quinn was left only with that odour on the attacker's fingers Jeannie Craig mentioned. If that failed to be a common factor, he was faced with the stark fact that this was either the work of one of the audience who could not be identified, or equally that it was a completely random attack.

'The maid described it as neither pleasant nor unpleasant,' Jarrett said. 'It is probably the badge of his trade, like the scent on a fishmonger or horse dealer.'

'All I can do is go back to Megan Speirs and Grace Martin,' Tommy Quinn suggested. 'If it jogs their memories, there are three other cases on record going back several months.'

'Delegate that, Sergeant,' Jarrett said quickly. 'Instruct Williamson to make those enquiries. I have other plans for you.'

'Sir?'

'I want you to call upon your maid, Netta. There is something I need that requires her assistance.'

'Is this regarding Mrs Bisley, Superintendent?'

'Very much so. If my memory serves me, a few hairs are enough to detect the presence of arsenic if it has been administered over a period. Somehow, and I leave the exact details up to you, I want you to obtain samples of Mrs Bisley's hair.'

It was a slightly bemused Sergeant Quinn who left the office then, first to locate Williamson, then to make his way to Alder Avenue.

* * *

Netta Byrne reflected surprise when she drew open the door and found Sergeant Quinn waiting on the top step.

'Tommy,' she said softly. 'Come in before someone sees you. They'll all be talking about this household.'

'Let them talk.' He jerked his head in the general direction of the interior of the house. 'Who's around?'

'Only Mrs Bisley, but she's upstairs in bed.

255

And Mrs Robbins in the kitchen, of course.'

'Miss Healey?'

'Gone to fetch Mrs Bisley's magazines. That should be my job, but I've the door to see to.'

'How long will she be gone?'

'Oh, about twenty minutes or so.' Netta cocked her head in a way that implied mild distrust. 'You're still up to something, aren't you?'

'I suppose I am.' Tommy placed his hands on her shoulders and hoped he looked sufficiently serious to obtain her cooperation. 'Look, Netta, you are devoted to your mistress, aren't you?'

'Of course. I don't like him at all, as you know, but Mrs Bisley has been good to me. If anything happened to her — '

'That is precisely the point. I want you to help me save her life.'

'I don't understand what you mean.'

'Then tell me this. Who brushes her hair?'

'I do. I always have done.'

'So no one would be surprised if you fetched the hairbrush.'

'What for?'

'You wash it, don't you?'

'Yes, in ammonia and water, but I did that just two days ago.'

'Then pretend to do it again, and hurry up

256

before Miss Healey gets back.'

Netta shook her head adamantly.

'Not until you tell me what this is all about,' she said firmly. 'You're not making any sense, Tommy.'

'Very well.' Despite what Superintendent Jarrett had said about not telling the girl the truth, there now seemed to be no other way of earning her trust. 'If you value Mrs Bisley's life you will do what I ask now.'

'Just one good reason.'

'We think she may be in danger and only a scientific test will prove whether we are right or wrong.'

She stared at him, her eyes widening in horror.

'You think she's being poisoned, don't you?' she breathed.

'I didn't say that.'

'You didn't have to. I'm not daft, you know. I've read about these things. It's the hair on the brush you want.'

'Yes it is. Now will you get it?'

'Is it him? Is it Bisley himself?'

'I can't say at this stage. But please hurry.'

13

Chief Constable Rattray's brief holiday had done him no good at all. He might have hoped that his many problems would disappear in his absence, and that he would return to a clean sheet and an easy life, but if anything things were even worse. And the Fates had still not finished with him. Even his intention to carpet Henry Jarrett for the singular lack of progress in the Western Bank robbery came to nothing when the superintendent placed the locket on the CC's desk and handed him Dr Hamilton's report.

'This is a result of the Marsh test on these strands of hair, sir,' he said confidently. 'They were taken from Seraphina Bisley's hairbrush. In Dr Hamilton's opinion there must be enough arsenic in her body to bring her close to death. As things stand, sir, it is just a matter of time.'

It was quite some time before Rattray spoke. When he finally did he was shaking with anger.

'Thought he would make a bloody fool of me, did he?' he said to no one in particular. He had quite obviously taken it personally for no reason that the chief of detectives could ascertain. 'Bring him in, Jarrett, and for God's sake get a confession.'

★ ★ ★

Alexander Bisley was clearly stunned as he took a seat at the interrogation table and stared at Henry Jarrett. Occasionally, his eyes drifted to the bland and unrevealing face of Charlie Grant, but for the most part his concern was with the senior officer.

'I don't understand, Superintendent,' he said. 'How could you possibly think that I would kill my own mother?'

'It would be the logical next step, Mr Bisley,' Jarrett informed him. 'After all, you murdered your uncle, Jacob French.'

'But that is preposterous. I have never hurt anyone in my life, let alone killed them.'

'Do you deny purchasing three shillings' worth of arsenic from McConnell the Chemist?'

'No, I don't deny it. I bought the powder to deal with a rat infestation in the cellar of the Commodore Hotel.'

'Which you told Mr McConnell was your hotel, when in fact it was owned by your uncle.'

'It was as good as mine.' Bisley clasped his

hands together in a defensive manner that was not lost on the detectives. 'My uncle had been ill for quite some time, so everything was left for me to do. I leave the house early in the morning and often don't get home until late. Since it was clear that there would be no betterment for him, I was generally accepted as being the proprietor of the hotel in all but name.'

'But he was taking his time over dying, wasn't he, Mr Bisley?' Jarrett suggested, shocking the arrested man to the very core. 'That was awkward, because although you had all the responsibilities, the Jacob French fortune remained outwith your reach.'

'I'll admit that the financial situation made it much more difficult,' Bisley replied. 'The costs of running a successful hotel are high, and things are only made worse when you have to go cap-in-hand for every sovereign. Even the monthly bills from the Fruit and Meat Markets had to be scrutinized and approved by a man who was very often *non compos mentis*. His doctor would tell me to come back later, when he might be able to comprehend.'

'It must have been very difficult for you, Mr Bisley.' Henry Jarrett agreed. 'It is hardly surprising that you should devise a very interesting solution to your problem.'

'I know that's what you believe, but after exhuming my uncle without my permission and finding nothing untoward, I thought you would have let the matter rest.' Bisley shook his head grimly. 'You seem to have a bee in your bonnet about this, Superintendent, but I did not poison Jacob French.'

'No, I know you didn't, but you are poisoning your mother. That was your plan all along, Mr Bisley, was it not? Considering Jacob French's condition, the police doctor is of the opinion that his death could quite easily be brought about by a fright. Exactly how you did this remains to be seen, but that was the clever part of it. You knew that once the authorities had made fools of themselves by undertaking an exhumation that proved fruitless, they would not wish the embarrassment of a repeat performance. Thus you were entirely free to kill your mother and inherit everything. In fact, you were so confident of success that you bought all of the arsenic from one shop and signed for it with your own name.'

'Naturally I used my own name. Only someone intent on an evil act would use an alias.'

'No, Mr Bisley, you signed the poisons book in your own name because if anything did go wrong there would be no defence against prosecution if you had used a fake one. I'm bound to say that it shows a wicked and calculating mind. Put quite simply, you murdered your uncle and intended to proceed to murder your mother after planning the whole thing meticulously.'

Alexander Bisley's eyes were wide with horror.

'Good God, that is the most dreadful thing I have ever heard,' he whispered hoarsely. 'How could anyone commit a horrible crime like that?'

'You tell us, Mr Bisley. Does the desire for money know any bounds? Do you honestly think that this is the first time someone has set out to murder a parent for gain? Numerous ruling houses throughout history made it something of an art form.'

'Yes, but I love my mother and would sooner die myself than harm her in any way.'

'Let us approach this from a different angle, Mr Bisley,' Charlie Grant put in. 'If you are not gradually using your three shillings' worth of arsenic on Seraphina Bisley, what did you do with it?'

'I told you. I put it down to destroy the rats.'

'Put it down how?'

'On lumps of sausage meat. I placed a quantity of this meat close to where I thought they entered the cellar and doctored them with arsenic. It was the first time I had ever used the substance, but I was assured by several people that it is most effective.'

'So you used all of the arsenic in this way?'

'Every last particle.'

'What did you do with McConnell's printed envelope?'

'I can't remember. Discarded it, I think.'

'In the cellar? Or would you have taken it away with you?'

'I really don't know. I probably threw it on the floor. Anyway, it is a mere detail. Hardly matters.'

'Who else could go down to this particular cellar?'

'No one. I have locked it and carry the key with me. There is another cellar which is used for wine, but it does not have a rat problem, perhaps because I had it repaired a few years ago.' By now, Bisley was wringing his hands in desperation. 'Please, Superintendent, I don't see why you can't believe me.'

'I don't believe you, Mr Bisley, because someone has been administering arsenic to your mother for some time now. According to my information, you visit Mrs Bisley in her sick room every evening when you get home. I think it would be fairly obvious to just about anyone that you are slowly poisoning her on those occasions. A forbidden confection, perhaps? A tiny amount of arsenic in each sweetie? Is it a little secret between you? I am sure that we could find these titbits if we looked.'

'Utter nonsense.' Bisley shook his head vehemently. 'This story of yours is nothing more than a complete fabrication.'

'We'll see, shall we?' Jarrett said flatly. 'But for the moment let us consider this business about the rats in the cellar. For all I know you may have acted out your scheme by feeding them a few lumps of sausage meat, or whatever, or you might not even have gone that far. You could just be making up the whole cellar story. One thing I am sure of was that the arsenic had always been intended for quite another purpose altogether.'

'You can't begin to prove any of this. Anyway, you have no grounds for obtaining a warrant to search my premises.'

'I don't need one.' The superintendent let this sink in. 'Whether we like it or not, responsibility for inspecting properties in which people dwell temporarily or permanently has fallen to the City of Glasgow Police. By concocting this yarn about rats you have effectively invited the police surgeon and me to visit your premises.'

Bisley tugged his handkerchief from his

breast pocket and dabbed his reddening forehead.

'Are you arresting me?' he asked lamely.

'For the time being I am going to detain you for further enquiries.' Jarrett held out an open palm. 'The key to the cellar, Mr Bisley. I think I would like to take a look at it now.'

★ ★ ★

Dr Hamilton's carriage arrived at the forecourt of the Commodore Hotel to find Superintendent Jarrett and Inspector Grant waiting by the wagonette. But before embarking on this current mission, the good doctor had other news to impart. It concerned a short length of purple thread that was tightly wrapped around the screw of the scissors used to kill Vincent Gittens, identified now as a very fine, but strong silk, which Dr Hamilton believed had been dyed using fuchsine. The finished effect was vibrant and garish, and ideally suited public performers and the like, but was not considered to be in good taste by ladies who knew about such things.

'It rather looks, Superintendent,' he said, 'that you may not be finished with Miss Amelia Moffat just yet.'

Charlie Grant took possession of the tiny

265

glass phial containing the incriminating strands.

'With your permission, Superintendent,' he said, 'I think I could be better employed attending to those two beauties. I don't really think you need me here.'

'As you wish, Inspector, but you had better take a couple of detective constables to assist the arrest and keep an eye on your back, all things considered.'

When Grant had departed, Jarrett and Dr Hamilton, along with a uniform to do the dirty work, made their way through the foyer of the hotel to the rear stairs which led down to a storage area where the doors to the cellars could be found. Little resistance was encountered and it was quite clear that Bisley was not one for delegating responsibility. Even the manager, Mr Jenkins, was little more than a figurehead and made no attempt to impede them.

Not that either Jarrett or Dr Hamilton really expected to find anything that would either incriminate or clear Alexander Bisley. It was merely a line that had to be followed.

On reaching the foot of the stone steps to the cellar Bisley claimed had been rat infested, they stood back and allowed the uniformed constable to evenly play the broad beam of his bulls-eye lamp over the dusty floor. Several bricks lay here and there from the original construction of the hotel some fifty years earlier, along with a few planks of grey, tinder-dry wood and small piles of rock-hard mortar. Otherwise, the large, low room was entirely unchanged and unused.

It would have been too much to ask of the rats to have left even the tiniest piece of sausage meat, but from Dr Hamilton's limited experience of such things he did anticipate finding the odd dead rat or two. But even there he was going to be disappointed. Not that the lack of a rodent corpse would make the slightest difference. A decent advocate, after taking advice on such matters and casting doubt on Dr Hamilton's expertise regarding vermin extermination, could and would drive a coach and horses through the prosecution's argument.

Then the lamp's yellow beam settled on a small paper envelope on which McConnell's name was beautifully printed in a spidery copperplate font. This was swiftly collected and placed within a larger sample bag which the good doctor then squirreled away in his black case.

'I'm afraid your hope of a conviction is about to go up in smoke,' Hamilton said. 'I am going to have to give evidence to the extent that the only packet of arsenic Bisley purchased from McConnell appears to have been used for exactly the purpose he claims.'

'He clearly transferred the poison to another packet and left this here as a decoy,' Jarrett offered.

'I have no doubt that it happened exactly that way, but do you really think a jury will believe that for a moment, Superintendent? It sounds perfectly feasible right here, and Bisley is certainly smart enough to leave the envelope for us to find, but I am bound to say that in a court of law it would sound as though you were grasping at straws. On the principle that the simplest explanation is normally the case, they would prefer to believe that Mr Bisley used up his three shillings' worth of arsenic on the rats and discarded the envelope right here. Any other explanation will not work.'

* * *

Charlie Grant was in no mood to be set back on the defensive yet again by the forceful and overprotective Amelia Moffat, particularly as he was accompanied on this occasion by DCs Williamson and Russell. It also helped that Miss Moffat was dressed in a subdued green, which served to diminish her in size.

'Inspector Grant,' she began, but that was

as far as her opening gambit got.

'The purple dress, Miss Moffat,' Grant said sharply. 'Where is it, please?'

Since that was the last thing she expected, Amelia Moffat was momentarily at a loss for a reply. Above her on the gantry, Eusebius Beck likewise reflected confusion.

'May I ask why?' the lady asked after a few moments.

'Just tell me where it is, if you don't mind, Miss Moffat.'

'In the costume trunk. If you give me a moment I'll get it for you.'

'No, don't bother. Just say where it is and DC Williamson will get it.'

She half-turned then, and waved a hand in the direction of a painted flat that was someone's notion of an Arabia that existed only in children's books.

'It is behind that,' she said.

A couple of minutes later Ian Williamson re-emerged from behind the minarets and flying carpets, only now he was carrying the purple dress over one arm and a grim metal corset that would not have been out of place in a torture chamber.

Charlie Grant accepted the steel girdle and drew out the long thin wires that were tightly affixed to various parts of it. He then returned this object to DC Williamson and accepted the dress instead. Here and there tiny holes in the purple material were ringed with copper eyelets.

'Presumably,' he said, 'the wires from that object pass through these holes and thence to the overhead walk and permit you to levitate.'

'Inspector Grant,' Beck called down from above, 'I am not aware of any law against magic and conjuring.'

'There is if the intention is to deceive and defraud.'

'Don't all conjurers deceive?'

'I think you know what I mean.' Charlie Grant laid the dress over the back of one of the chairs. 'But I'm not interested in your swindling ways. I am still investigating the murder of Vincent Gittens.'

'I was under the impression that we had told you all we know about that man's unfortunate demise,' Miss Moffat stated flatly. 'What more can we possibly say?'

'Well, you might like to explain how a thread from that dress came to be twisted around the screw of the scissors used in the unlawful killing.'

For a few moments, silence reigned, then Amelia Moffat said, 'You said nothing about this before, Inspector. I can only conclude that it isn't true.'

'Oh, it's true, all right, Miss Moffat, and it

is all we need to hang you for Gittens's murder.' After a brief silence, Charlie Grant said, 'You have one way out and one only. If you confess to killing Gittens to protect yourself or another party, the fact that you have not profited in any way from his death should bring in a manslaughter verdict at worst.'

'And at best?'

'You could walk free, but that would depend on how many character witnesses you could persuade to speak on your behalf.'

Miss Moffat clasped her hands together on her abdomen and adopted a prim, schoolmistress look that would serve her well in a court of law.

'That man,' she said, 'attempted to extort money from the Professor, and when Mr Beck properly refused to pay up he viciously attacked him, seizing him by the shirt and threatening to beat him. As you can see, Professor Beck is not a strong man.'

Charlie Grant could have pointed out that he was obviously strong enough to climb up on the gantry, and — if Superintendent Jarrett was correct — transport a corpse quite some distance in a wheelbarrow. But since he would settle quite nicely for a quick conclusion, leaving it to the Fiscal to consider the self-defence plea, he saw no reason to scare them off now.

'A couple of points,' he said. 'First, did you know about the money on Gittens's person?'

'Of course we knew, Inspector,' Miss Moffat stated. 'We are not thieves, you know, no matter what you may think of us.'

'Second question, why did you dump the body on Glasgow Green?'

'We didn't know he was dead. That was why we left the scissors in place. We didn't want him to bleed to death, whatever sort of man he was.'

Charlie Grant smiled at this. Good answer, he thought. Professor Beck could do a lot worse than have Amelia Moffat for a friend.

'Is that the way of it?' he asked. 'Are you willing to sign a confession declaring that you killed Vincent Gittens in self-defence?'

'Yes, Inspector,' Miss Moffat said, 'I am. That's how it was.'

'And you further admit that the killing took place in Mr Beck's lodgings?' When no reply was forthcoming, Charlie went on, 'This is no time to be concerned for your reputation, Miss Moffat. Being mindful of the way such dubious matters can influence a jury, your lawyer will no doubt explain that you were there to make alterations to your stage clothes, as I believe they are called. That would also explain why you had the scissors to hand.'

'That is exactly right, Inspector,' Miss Moffat said, having nodded her agreement to his every word. 'That individual must have followed us, and almost as soon as we were inside the Professor's rooms he appeared at the door with his aggressive, threatening way.'

Charlie Grant raised a hand to silence her.

'Save it for your lawyer, Miss Moffat,' he said. 'It isn't good to over-rehearse.'

★ ★ ★

Sergeant Quinn had made no definite plans to see Netta Byrne again, assuming that his presence at the theatre merely served as a convenient substitute for Harold the driver. After all, his company and her information represented a suitable trade-off. But Superintendent Jarrett had decided otherwise. Rather than risk having a search warrant refused on the grounds of insufficient evidence, not to mention the Necropolis disaster, he chose instead to make use of the maid's devotion to her mistress and her dislike of Alexander Bisley.

'I hope you realize that Mrs Bisley mustn't know that her son has been detained,' Tommy advised when they were together in the hallway at Rosebank House. Fortunately, Miss Healey was enjoying a lie-down, rendering his planned excuse quite unnecessary. 'I am advised that the shock could kill her.'

Netta was naturally concerned and somewhat apprehensive about searching Mr Bisley's rooms, which comprised the top floor and were out of bounds. Apart from changing the linen and keeping the apartment dust-free and tidy, she rarely had cause to pause on that level when retiring to her own attic quarters which she shared with Mrs Robbins.

'Mrs Bisley will hear me up above,' she whispered even though there was no need. 'I'm only up there in the morning and last thing at night.'

'Then tip-toe.'

'Easier said than done.' Netta frowned as she thought of having to talk her way out of a very difficult situation. 'What is it you want me to look for?'

'We think it might be confectionary. Possibly a box or tin. But whatever you do, don't eat any of it.'

'What do you think I am?' She gave him a dirty look, then added, 'Are you sure it's somewhere in his rooms?'

'No, we can't be sure, but the superintendent believes that Bisley wouldn't leave anything like that in the sick room and he is not likely to carry it back and forward to the hotel each day.'

'But if it is up there, won't it be under lock and key?'

'Almost certainly.' Tommy Quinn produced a thin strip of metal from his waistcoat pocket and held it up for her to see. 'One of Superintendent's acquisitions.'

'What is it?'

'A pick-lock.' Tommy grinned at her. 'And you might like to bring that African mask you mentioned.'

* * *

When Alexander Bisley was brought back up from the cells in the white-tiled basement at headquarters, his slouching shuffle spoke volumes. He knew they had found what they were looking for and that further lying would be counter-productive. Unless he wished to dig his own grave with his mouth, it was time for cooperation.

Jarrett opened the square tin and showed him the contents. It was a quite unnecessary gesture, apart from demonstrating that it wasn't a bluff. They really had discovered the confectionary in the bottom drawer of his writing bureau.

'They are called marzipan logs, I believe,'

275

Jarrett said. 'Did you make them yourself, Mr Bisley?'

Bisley nodded.

'In the hotel kitchen. Easily done. Uncooked marzipan.'

'Doctor Hamilton tells me that the one he examined contained a small quantity of arsenic, so I presume they all do.' Superintendent Jarrett grinned at him. 'I was going to ask you to try one, but since you are plainly being obliging there is really no need.'

Bisley smiled sardonically.

'Would you accept the explanation that it was intended for the rats?' he asked.

'No.'

'In that case, Superintendent, I think it is time that I had legal representation.'

'So do I, Mr Bisley, and I sincerely hope you have sufficient funds of your own to pay for the very best, because otherwise you are going to have to ask your mother to underwrite your defence, and I don't think even you could be that perverse.'

Ever since he returned to the interrogation room, Alexander Bisley's eyes had been repeatedly drawn to the tribal mask lying at the end of the table, beside a wooden writing tray with its paper, ink well and dipping pen. So far no mention had been made of the mask, despite its colourful, contorted and terrifying countenance, and the fact that Jarrett had found it sufficiently important to bring along. Yet both of them knew perfectly well that it had been taken from Bisley's room, so for him to fail to remark on it was tantamount to admitting his guilt, and the longer he waited the better it was for the superintendent.

'A strange object,' Bisley said. 'Scary.'

'I doubt if it would frighten a child,' Jarrett replied, 'but in subdued light who can say what effect it could have on a very sick man, especially if he was drifting between consciousness and delirium.'

Bisley nodded. He was smiling thinly.

'You are wasting your time, you know,' he said. 'You could never prove it in a million years.'

'I wouldn't have to if you would do the decent thing and confess.'

'And hang for a dying man? I hardly think so, Superintendent.'

'The alternative is life in Bridewell for the attempted murder of your mother.'

'Oh, I don't think it will come to that. A lesser crime, perhaps?'

'Being?'

'Let us say I believed my mother to be seriously ill and wished to be a merciful son.'

'People wishing to be merciful in such

terrible cases do not use arsenic, Mr Bisley.'

'Nevertheless, would you accept such an outcome?'

'It isn't up to me. The Fiscal will decide that you should face a charge of attempted murder, and after that it would be up to you and your advocate to persuade the jury that you were driven by concern for your mother's condition.' Jarrett pushed the writing tray in front of the prisoner. 'If that is to be your statement please commit it to paper.'

Bisley nodded and lifted the pen.

14

It was the last thing the grizzled and rather stunned watchman expected at that time of the morning. After pulling on the heavy handle to open the sliding door a little, he finished the job by putting his shoulder to the upright and pushing the metal runner along its track far enough to admit the wagonette and a freshly-painted van into the pitted yard.

The breakthrough had come the night before, when Sergeant Quinn had finally found a pattern to the attacks. All of the girls were maids in households where improvements to the plumbing had recently taken place. And in each case the work was carried out by the firm of Benjamin Carney, Plumber and Gasfitter. To make absolutely sure, Jarrett and Mrs Maitland, with Lizzie following closely behind, had escorted Jeannie Craig up to the bathroom, where he had instructed the girl to compare the joint around the new geyser to the smell on the attackers hand. Her immediate recoil said it all. Lead solder.

'When does Carney usually get in?' Jarrett asked the old one.

'Any minute now.' The elderly watchman's

expression reflected the confusion he was experiencing within. 'What do you want him for?'

But this was ignored.

'How does he come?'

'On foot. He only lives up there in Sharpe's Lane.' The man was persistent if nothing else. 'I asked you what you wanted him for.'

Once again, it was as though he had never spoken. Instead, Jarrett instructed Tommy Quinn to make sure his men were out of sight when Carney arrived, because the last thing he wanted was a foot chase through the narrow alleyways and permanently sunless canyons that criss-crossed this entire warren of red brick factories and warehouses.

It was only a couple of minutes later that the first sound of studded boots on flagstones reached those who waited silently in the yard. As soon as Carney passed through the gate any possibility of a retreat was immediately blocked by a uniformed officer.

But escape was clearly not among the plumber's intentions.

'What the hell — '

'Benjamin Carney.' Jarrett stated, rather than asked. 'We want to talk to you about a number of serious assaults.'

Contrary to expectations, Carney reflected no great surprise.

'Does it have to be right now?' Carney asked. 'I've got a lot of work in hand and that assistant of mine has let me down.'

Jarrett glanced at Tommy Quinn, who merely shrugged.

'Explain,' the superintendent said. 'Who are you talking about?'

'Kenny Noone. Buggered off two days ago and left me in the lurch. I went round to his room in Hob's Wynd, but the landlord said he had packed a bag and vanished.' Carney looked from one to the other. 'Now, if you don't mind, I've got a lot to do.'

After two days there was little sense in watching the railway stations, so it was left to Tommy Quinn to send Noone's description to all police forces via the electric telegraph. The van, still unoccupied, returned to the stables behind Central, and Henry Jarrett, with PC Jamieson at the ribbons, set off in the wagonette for the relative boredom of the office.

At that point, he had no way of knowing what was waiting for him.

* * *

The end came swiftly for the Guardian of the Sacred Word. The onset of madness had been a slow, gradual affair, starting with a vague idea that he was in some way special, and progressing through an ever-deepening sense of absolute uniqueness to the point where it could no longer be doubted that he was the Chosen One.

He had probably lost much of his sanity even before the High Priest showed him the *tabots*, but it was the headlong dash for safety and escape from the temple precinct that convinced him of his special position in the great scheme of things. With every step he took his confidence grew, until he was risking life and limb in raging rivers and yawning chasms, and little by little leaving his pursuers far behind. Yet they were determined men, fired with fury at what he had done, and they halted only when he shot a fisherman and stole his boat. Already the first rains had begun and his timing merely demonstrated his superiority and right to possess these wonderful things.

But deep down he had always known that they would find him and that the end of his earthly stay must come, if only because nothing lasts forever and this he welcomed as part of God's design. He turned quickly at the first sound of a door crashing open and saw his manservant attempting to stop them reaching him, but a single thrust drove the curved blade of a *shotel* clean through the man's body and he arched backwards to crash on the floor. Then they were at the Guardian, stabbing repeatedly while he raised his arms and called upon Heaven to receive him.

What they had come for lay on the altar, each with its own gold and red cloth square. After they had carefully wrapped the holy relics, one of them snatched the gold lion that secured his cloak, while another tugged the lion claw dagger from his silk waistband. In moments they were gone, leaving behind them a household in screaming confusion.

★ ★ ★

Henry Jarrett sat bolt upright in the wagonette as Charlie Grant and Ian Williamson emerged swiftly from the main door to headquarters. PC Jamieson had no need to bring Domino to a complete standstill, because the inspector tugged open the low door and both jumped in while the carriage was still on the move.

'Parkfield House,' Grant called, then turned to his superintendent. 'We've just had a message on the electric telegraph from the Gorbals Police, sir. Cyrus Brand and his servant have been done to death.'

'By?'

'No one knows. I would venture to guess that all hell has broken out in that house, so it's surprising that anyone had the presence of mind to call us.'

★ ★ ★

The communication had not been strictly accurate. The tall dark-skinned man was dead, certainly, but Brand, despite numerous wounds, still hung on to the last vestige of life. It would seem that his desire to die was not quite as strong as he had at first thought. When Jarrett and Grant, closely followed by DC Williamson, forced their way through the gawping servants, who were now leaderless and dumbly waiting guidance, he still clutched the rim on the altar and watched through flickering eyes as they approached him.

'Can you understand me, Mr Brand?' Jarrett asked.

'Perfectly, but you had better be quick, Superintendent. Time, as they say, is of the essence.'

'Do you know who did it?'

'Not by name, but they probably had right on their side.'

'The King's Abyssinians?'

'Who else?'

Jarrett probably had more questions than Brand had time, so it had to be the most pressing.

'What was Hadden made to reveal?' he asked.

'The names of his cohorts.'

'Why?'

Brand smiled thinly.

'They despoiled the *tabots*. They touched them with their bare hands.'

'And that was sufficient reason to kill them?'

'Of course.' Brand's whisper was even fainter now. 'No one touches that which God has touched and is permitted to live.'

'One still does.'

'God will finish the task. I have done my best.'

Jarrett wanted to know many things, but knew he might have to settle for just one answer that had been troubling him.

'How did you find out who had robbed the bank?' he asked.

'Only the lion was missing.' Brand was having difficulty keeping his eyes on one spot now. 'I offered a high reward in the next day's paper. He responded by the afternoon's mail and made arrangements to meet me. It was so easy.'

'Did he tell you if he had planned the robbery?'

But the eyes were still forever now and the fingers had lost their ability to grip. Jarrett, who had been on one knee before the altar, rose and indicated the sea of faces.

'Better get their statements, Inspector,' he said. 'Or at least those who witnessed something.'

'Certainly, sir.' Grant gestured to Williamson. 'Get their statements, lad, but don't waste all day on it.'

Superintendent Henry Jarrett, for his part, had just answered his own question. As soon as he heard himself speak the words, and knew that Brand was never going to be able to reply, the truth about Christopher Hadden's grim death hit him.

★   ★   ★

Had he arrived just a few minutes later, Jarrett would have missed Charlotte Stuart entirely. As it was, the Langfield Mansion in West Regent Street was now a hollow shell. Apart from a few select pieces, its ornate furnishings and carpets had been packed and sent to the auctioneers. Of the staff, only the small wizened retainer remained, and he was about to retire and be a pest to an obliging niece somewhere in Lanarkshire. But he would not be departing until he had attended to the front door for the final time.

Henry Jarrett had not expected this, but at the same time was not entirely surprised.

'A sudden decision, Mrs Stuart?' he asked.

'Not really.' She had been waiting in the now empty and oversized hallway with just a couple of cases to take with her in the Hansom when it finally got there. Everything else that she was keeping had gone on ahead. 'I had always planned on spending my final years in warmer and more luxurious surroundings. Christopher's death merely brought it forward.'

'So you are not returning?'

'Hardly. Too far and no reason.'

'And the property?'

'I have instructed Hillyard and Palmer, my house agents, to sell the house and transfer the money to me.'

'In British Guiana?'

Charlotte Stuart smiled.

'Very good, Superintendent,' she said. 'Yes, I have a plantation in Port Seba on the Demerara River. But you already knew that, didn't you?'

'When I mentioned it before I assumed you were unaware of the place, Mrs Stuart.'

'Precisely, you assumed. I didn't actually say that I had never heard of it. I said that Christopher would not flee the country.'

'But you would?'

'I'm not fleeing, Superintendent. As I said, it was all part of my plan.'

'Like the robbery.' Jarrett paused briefly, then said, 'The perfectly placed shop, a brother who had recently retired from the Royal Engineers, and through him access to men who could carry your scheme through in a way that no petty criminals could. How long did it take to formulate the plan, Mrs Stuart — ten seconds? Less? Or perhaps it sprang fully formed into your thoughts like Athena from the head of Zeus.'

'I really don't know what you are talking about, Superintendent Jarrett.' Charlotte Stuart consulted the tiny Lepine lady's watch that hung on her chest like a medal. 'If you intend to do anything but talk, I suggest you get a move on. My ship sails with the tide.'

'I could impound your luggage at the quay until it has been thoroughly searched. You certainly wouldn't be sailing on this vessel, if you ever sail at all.'

'No, I don't think you could do that without a great deal more evidence than you actually have. If indeed you have any at all.' Mrs Stuart waved in the direction of the door. The Hansom was coming and there was no reason to prolong this conversation. 'Anyway, sir, I think you must realize in your

288

heart of hearts that you wouldn't find anything.'

'Because it is already on the high seas, you mean?'

'Goodbye, Superintendent,' she said warmly. 'I doubt that you will ever find your way to Port Seba, so we are unlikely to meet again.'

'You may be right, Mrs Stuart,' Jarrett admitted, 'but doesn't it trouble you in the slightest that he probably died rather than tell ruthless murderers who was behind the robbery?'

'Really, sir,' she said as she moved to the top step and watched the arrival of the cab. 'I am not quite sure what you mean by robbery. I have never stolen anything in my life.'

'Not personally, no, but you did orchestrate the largest theft in banking history. Most of those who suffered loss have refused to reveal exactly the nature of their property, or how they obtained it, but those who have done admit to a loss in excess of a million pounds. The real total may be several times that. Quite enough to buy you a city in British Guiana, Mrs Stuart.'

'I suppose it would.' Charlotte Stuart descended to the broad pavement and paused while the driver jumped down and opened the door for her. Then he stowed the luggage and regained his seat.

Jarrett waited until the Hansom was out of sight before crossing to the wagonette and climbing in.

'Back to headquarters, PC Jamieson,' he said flatly.

'Are we not having a good day, sir?'

'Just do it.' Jarrett frowned at his boots. 'And just because you're the only one who can handle that creature doesn't mean you're indispensable.'

'Doesn't it, sir? Here's me thinking that's exactly what it meant.'

* * *

It was close to 6 p.m. when the electric telegraph operator at the end of the hall waved across to Tommy Quinn, who scurried first to collect the pencilled message, then directly to Superintendent Jarrett.

'Kenny Noone has been detained by the Edinburgh police,' he said quickly. 'They had notified all the plumbers that he might be looking for work.'

'Good thinking,' Jarrett replied. 'And?'

'That's the problem, sir. What he told them just doesn't fit with what we thought to be the case.'

'Well, come on, man. It is getting dangerously close to dinner.'

'In that case, I will try to be brief. According to Noone, Benjamin Carney told him that the police were after him for a number of attacks on girls. It seems that the boy was fined twenty shillings for stealing lead off church roofs a couple of years ago and Judge Findlay warned him that he faced a custodial sentence if he ever came up in front of him again for any reason. The problem is, Noone swears he didn't have anything to do with the girls, but was too scared to stay around and be rushed into the clink.'

'Had you made enquiries about young Noone?'

'No, sir. I had no reason to until the matter of the lead solder arose.'

'So why would Carney tell him that?'

'I don't know, Superintendent, but it didn't end there. Benjamin Carney gave him four pounds and told him to leave the city for good. It was his only chance, he said, because the police were determined to hang it on someone and he was the perfect candidate.'

'Did he indeed?' Jarrett closed his eyes then and recalled what Mrs Maitland had told him about the day the gas geyser arrived. They were mismatched, the plumber and his assistant, she said, because the boy was left-handed and was heaving the heavy thing one way, while Carney's inclination was the opposite. 'It didn't register with me at the time, Sergeant, but Jeannie Craig told me that the attacker had placed the knife point under her right ear. What does that suggest to you?'

Tommy Quinn lifted the superintendent's ruler in his left hand and turned it this way and that, but it was awkward and quite difficult to manipulate. Even his wrist was at a silly angle.

'Noone would have clasped his right hand over her mouth,' he said. 'The point of the knife would have been under the left ear. Even if he had tried to bring it right round to the other side his right hand would have been in the way.'

'Inspector Grant has gone off for a spot of well-earned rest,' Jarrett said, fishing out his half-hunter and comparing it to the wall clock. 'But you are an energetic young fellow, so you won't mind a bit of overtime. You might start by telling Edinburgh to release Kenny Noone, then I am sure you won't object to bringing in Benjamin Carney.'

'Not in any way, sir. It'll be my pleasure.'

★ ★ ★

It was one of those irritating coincidences. The Hansom cab had been closely following the wagonette ever since it turned into Highfield Road, and now both vehicles were drawing to a halt in front of 76 Delmont Avenue. Henry Jarrett opened the low door and stepped out onto what was very probably the cleanest section of pavement in the West End, just as Albert Sweetman alighted from the public conveyance.

'Ah, Jarrett,' the overweight salesman said by way of greeting. 'What a trip that was. Made more sales and collected more money in the Borders than I did in the rest of the country.'

'I am very pleased to hear that, Mr Sweetman,' the superintendent said, 'because it may be more important than you realize.'

'Really? How's that?'

'Correct me if I'm wrong, but I think I remember your mentioning the acquisition of a new agency. The Etna range, I believe.'

'Excellent products, and I am the sole distributor in the city.'

'Which must mean that you supplied Benjamin Carney and Company.'

'Indeed I did. Twenty Etna gas geysers in the last three months. As a matter of fact, I am going to request payment in full in the morning.'

'Which brings me to the awkward bit,' Jarrett confided. 'I just arrested him.'

What ought to have been the near-silent tranquility of a suburban evening was broken by the slow, leaden shuffling of Albert Sweetman making for the front door with two oversized sample cases.

'Now, that wasn't very nice, sir,' PC Jamieson observed.

But Jarrett wasn't listening.

'Roast gigot of mutton, served with rich gravy and boiled potatoes,' he said.

'And the same to you, sir.'

The Hansom had already covered a good half of the distance to Highfield Road when Jamieson set Domino off in pursuit. Henry Jarrett closed the garden gate and enjoyed a few quiet moments on the top step, until the sounds of iron-rimmed wheels and trotting hooves had finally faded into the distance, then he stepped inside, slid the chain onto its keeper and left the world outside.

We do hope that you have enjoyed reading this large print book.

Did you know that all of our titles are available for purchase?

We publish a wide range of high quality large print books including:
Romances, Mysteries, Classics
General Fiction
Non Fiction and Westerns

Special interest titles available in large print are:
The Little Oxford Dictionary
Music Book
Song Book
Hymn Book
Service Book

Also available from us courtesy of Oxford University Press:
Young Readers' Dictionary
(large print edition)
Young Readers' Thesaurus
(large print edition)

For further information or a free brochure, please contact us at:
Ulverscroft Large Print Books Ltd.,
The Green, Bradgate Road, Anstey,
Leicester, LE7 7FU, England.
Tel: (00 44) 0116 236 4325
Fax: (00 44) 0116 234 0205

JUPITER'S GOLD

Guy Fraser

1863. It all begins with the murder of a customs officer and in the days to follow there will be others. Apart from the mode of their deaths there seems little to connect them. Superintendent Jarrett, Inspector Grant and Sergeant Quinn of the Detective Department at Glasgow Central must also contend with upper-class thieves targeting jewellery shops, and an archaeologist with a taste for the high life. Are these crimes linked? And why does a worthless lump of stone attract the attention of ruthless men who will stop at nothing to locate the hiding place of Jupiter's Gold?

BLADE OF THE ASSASSIN

Guy Fraser

1863. The Detective Department at Glasgow Central is undermanned and short of funds, yet Superintendent Jarrett, Inspector Grant and Sergeant Quinn are expected to run to ground a multiple murderer, a vengeful madman and a professional pornographer. Henry Jarrett depends solely on deduction, whilst Inspector Charlie Grant brings to bear his experience of the city's back streets. Tommy Quinn for his part is at home with the recently introduced technologies of crime scene photography and the electric telegraph. Together, they uncover a huge conspiracy — the proportions of which could shake the political administrations on both sides of the Atlantic.

THE CUCKOO CLOCK SCAM

Roger Silverwood

Detective Inspector Angel investigates the murder of millionaire film writer and producer, Peter Santana. His body has been found in a lonely farmhouse where he used to hide himself away to write. There, strangely, Angel finds a dead pig in a silk nightdress in Santana's bed. Further investigations become more mystifying when he realises that wherever he makes an inquiry a cuckoo clock hangs upon the wall. The South Yorkshire town of Bromersley has cuckoo clocks everywhere. The DI and his team race to solve the murder, prevent more mayhem and unravel the mystery of the cuckoo clock scam . . .